Edward L. Cutts

Saint Jerome

Edward L. Cutts

Saint Jerome

ISBN/EAN: 9783741190551

Manufactured in Europe, USA, Canada, Australia, Japa

Cover: Foto ©Andreas Hilbeck / pixelio.de

Manufactured and distributed by brebook publishing software
(www.brebook.com)

Edward L. Cutts

Saint Jerome

The Fathers for English Readers.

SAINT JEROME.

BY

REV. EDWARD L. CUTTS, B.A.,

HON. D.D. UNIV. OF THE SOUTH, U.S.A.; AUTHOR OF "TURNING POINTS OF ENGLISH CHURCH HISTORY," ETC.

FOURTH EDITION.

PUBLISHED UNDER THE DIRECTION OF THE TRACT COMMITTEE.

LONDON:
SOCIETY FOR PROMOTING CHRISTIAN KNOWLEDGE,
NORTHUMBERLAND AVENUE, CHARING CROSS, W.C.
43, QUEEN VICTORIA STREET, E.C.
BRIGHTON: 129, NORTH STREET.
NEW YORK: E. & J. B. YOUNG & CO.
1897.

CONTENTS.

A 2

PREFACE TO THE SERIES.

WHILE all those who pretend to the character of educated people would be ashamed to be ignorant of the history of Greece and Rome, the lives and achievements of the great men of these countries, and the works of their chief writers, it is to be feared that they content themselves often with a very slight knowledge of the history of the Christian Church and of the illustrious ecclesiastics who have exercised so vast an influence upon the institutions and manners, the literature and philosophy, as well as the religion of modern Europe.

The series of volumes, of which the present forms one, is intended to present to ordinary English readers sketches of the Chief Fathers of the Church, their biographies, their works, and their times.

Those already prepared are—

THE APOSTOLIC FATHERS,
THE DEFENDERS OF THE FAITH (Apologists),
ST. AUGUSTINE,
ST. JEROME.

Others are in hand.

It is hoped that the series will supply the intelligent Churchman with a lively, accurate, and fairly complete view of the most important periods of Church history.

ST. JEROME.

CHAPTER I.

BIRTH AND EDUCATION OF JEROME.

A.D. 346-363.

IN the middle of the fourth century the city of
Aquileia was the capital of the province of Venetia,
and one of the grandest cities of Italy. It was situated at the northern bend of the Adriatic Sea, a little
eastward of the cluster of low islands upon which, a
century afterwards, its inhabitants, fleeing from the
invading Huns, founded modern Venice.

Lying on the one great highroad into Italy from
the side of Illyria and Pannonia, the city was a great
commercial emporium; while its situation, com
manding the whole country between the mountains
and the sea, made it of great military importance in
the defence of the peninsula; it was therefore strongly
fortified, and was the chief military station of the
north-east frontier of Italy.

Here, in the year 340 A.D., the younger Constantine
was defeated and slain, almost beneath the city walls,
and his brother Constans became emperor of the
undivided West. The place and the event serve to
mark the birth of the subject of this essay. The
exact situation of the village of Strido, the birthplace

of Jerome, is lost, but it is known that it was near
Aquileia, on the road which ran from that city north-
ward to Emona, and probably just at the point where
the road crosses over Mount Ocra, part of the chain
of the Julian Alps. The exact date of his birth is
uncertain, but it was most probably about six years
after the death of Constantine II. in the battle outside Aquileia.

In Strido, then, a suburban village of Aquileia,
about the year 346 A.D., Constans ruling the Empire
of the West from Milan, and Constantius, in Constantinople, ruling the Empire of the East, was born
Eusebius Hieronimus Sophronius, commonly known
to us by the modern form of his second name,
Jerome, the first, and the most learned and eloquent,
of the Fathers of the Latin Church.

He was probably of Dalmatian race. His father
possessed a small landed estate, and seems to have
been a person of respectable social position. He
had a brother, Paulinian, and a sister. Since, in the
biographical allusions which abound in his writings,
he nowhere mentions his mother, it is probable
that she died before he was old enough to remember
her. His family was Christian, and he was brought
up in the Christian faith ; but he was not baptized in
infancy. It was, at that period, a common practice,
though reprobated by the Church, to delay Baptism
till some spiritual crisis, or the approach of death,
under the idea that sin in the unbaptized was less
heinous, and that baptism would at length wash away
all the sins of the previous life. He was carefully
educated at home by a tutor ; and Bonosus, the son

of a rich neighbour, who seems to have been his foster-brother, and was the inseparable companion of his early years, was educated with him.

Thus he grew up into manhood amidst the local influences of a residence between the mountains and the sea—the Alps and the Adriatic; and under the social influences of the rude, energetic Dalmatian and Pannonian peasantry and farmers on one side, and on the other of the civilization of the neighbouring metropolis of the province.

The political and religious history of the period during which the boy was growing up into manhood was too remarkable not to have had an influence upon an ardent and talented youth. His boyhood from seven to fifteen was passed in the period in which Constantius, now by the death of his brother sole emperor, was endeavouring to coerce the Western Church into the acceptance of the Arianism long predominant in the East. The general persecution, the conduct of Liberius, Bishop of Rome, his brave resistance, his exile, the intrusion of Felix into the see, Liberius's acceptance of an ambiguous creed, his return, the schism between his party and that of Felix—these were questions which agitated Italian society, and were discussed in every Christian home. The Council of Rimini, "when the whole world groaned, and was astonished to find itself Arian," took place when Jerome was fourteen, and the words we have quoted are the record in after years of his own recollection of the event. Then came the death of Constantius, the accession of Julian, his apostasy, his endeavour to revive the belief in and the worship

of the ancient gods of Rome, his tragical death in
the Persian campaign, the succession of Jovian,
and the final triumph of Christianity—these were
the public events in the midst of which the youth
passed his fifteenth, sixteenth, and seventeenth years.
Jovian's short reign passed, and Valentinian sat on the
throne of the West, making Treves the Imperial residence, when, at the age of seventeen, Jerome was sent,
together with Bonosus, to complete his education at
Rome.

CHAPTER II.

ROME IN THE FOURTH CENTURY.

A.D. 363.

ROME in the fourth century was in the period of its very greatest extent and architectural magnificence. The series of public buildings and monuments with which a succession of emperors and great nobles had adorned the Mistress of the World—the temples, basilicas, palaces, forums, colonnades, triumphal arches, statues, theatres, baths, and gardens—had been completed by the triumphal arch with which Constantine commemorated his victory over Maxentius; and the whole series was still uninjured by time or violence.

And the city had lost, as yet, little of its ancient population and wealth and splendour. It is true it had ceased to be the seat of the world's government and the centre of the world's affairs. From the beginning of the reign of Diocletian (A.D. 277), that is, for a space of nearly a hundred years, the Emperors had ceased to reside in Rome. Under the new organization which that able statesman had given to the empire, the sovereigns no longer kept up the ancient forms of the Republic, under which the earlier Cæsars had decently veiled their power. They had found it desirable, for military reasons, to place the seats of Government at more convenient

centres, and politic to remove their courts from the
influence of the antique Republican spirit which still
survived in Rome, and from the rivalry of the great
patrician houses.   Constantine had built and adorned
Constantinople as the capital of the new empire ; and
when the Imperial authority was divided, the emperors of the West had chosen Milan for their residence, and had enlarged and adorned and fortified
the city till, in the words of a contemporary poet,
" it did not feel oppressed by the neighbouring greatness of Rome."[1]   In these new capitals of the East
and West the joint emperors exercised their absolute
rule ; took counsel only with advisers of their own
choice, made and unmade at pleasure the great
ministers of State, the governors of the provinces,
the generals of the armies ; surrounded themselves
with eunuchs and guards, and with the etiquette of
Eastern royalty, and the splendours of a parvenu
Court.   At Rome, meantime, the great patricians
still resided.   Left outside the new Imperial constitution, they on their part had held themselves aloof
from the new order of things.   They had not deserted
the city to swell the splendour of the new Courts, but
still occupied their vast palaces on the hills of Rome,
dignified with the busts of great ancestors, and
adorned with the spoils of provinces ; they still drew
immense revenues from the produce of estates and
the tribute of cities scattered over the Roman world.
If some of the great ancient families had been de-
stroyed or impoverished by the jealousy or cupidity

---

[1] Ansonius (A. D. 309-394).

of the Cæsars, new families had risen in their place, who, if they had a less noble ancestry, had wealth which enabled them to vie with the ancient families in ostentation, and who often supplied the lack of pedigree by imaginary claims of descent from the heroes of ancient story. These great houses still retained their numerous households of slaves, and still found employment for the traders and craftsmen of the city. The Senate, though deprived of all share in Imperial affairs, and reduced to the functions of the municipal government of Rome, still, from the rank of those who composed it and the great traditions which it inherited, retained something of its ancient prestige.

The poorer citizens had long ceased to enrol themselves in the legions; they disdained to exercise trade or handicraft; they clung to their faded dignity as Roman citizens; maintained existence by help of public doles, and spent their days in the taverns, the amphitheatres, the baths, and the public places.

It was but too natural that such a population, excluded from the ennobling occupations of the State, should fall into a life of luxury and dissipation. The contemporary historians give vivid pictures of the boundless prodigality and luxury of the nobles, their effeminacy, frivolity, and dissoluteness; and of the greed, corruption and turbulence of the mob.[1]

The religious condition of this population was re markable. The nobles had clung to the ancient gods of Rome as part of the old order of things, which had bequeathed to them their greatness, in opposition

[1] Ammianus Marcellinus describes the manners of Rome at this period: lib. 28, ch. viii. ix. x.

to Christianity, which, since Constantine, was an essential feature of the new order. The offices of Pontiff and Augur were still sought by the most illustrious members of the Senate, and " the dignity of their birth reflected additional splendour on their sacerdotal character. Their robes of purple, chariots of state, and sumptuous entertainments, attracted the attention of the people; and they received from the public revenue an ample stipend which liberally supported the splendour of the priesthood, and all the expenses of the worship of the State."[1] Many of the noble houses had hereditary cults, much as in later times the great mediæval families had their patron saints. The temples and shrines were still maintained, and the sacrifices and solemnities celebrated with all their accustomed pomp in Rome, while the provincial temples were mostly destitute of priest or sacrifice, and were falling into decay.

At the same time the Christians were numerous in the city, and the Church was well organized, wealthy, and influential. So long ago as the time of Diocletian, there were in Rome and its environs, twenty-five public churches and fifteen suburban basilicas connected with the catacombs. Constantine had given several new basilicas to the Church. And the number of the churches, and still more, the number of the priests, deacons, and minor officials of the Church, during nearly a century of freedom from persecution had, doubtless, greatly increased. What is specially notable is, that the female members of the noble families were generally Christian, even while their

---

[1] Gibbon, ch. xxviii.

fathers and brothers, husbands and sons, still refused the new faith. The voluntary donations of the wealthy members of the Christian body furnished the Church with ample revenues. The Bishop maintained a sumptuous establishment, and kept a table and an equipage, which rivalled those of the wealthy nobles. The clergy were received in the palaces of the Patriciate, and were enriched by the offerings of the wealthy members of their flocks. The influence of the Church was maintained among the lower class of the people, by a numerous and well-organized clergy, and fostered by the regular distribution of large charities.

This was the magnificent and luxurious, half pagan and half Christian, Rome, to which our young Dalmatian, with his foster-brother, came up as to a university to complete his education.

Emerging[2] from the defiles of the Sabine hills, upon a wide plain of coarse, luxuriant pasturage, dotted over with herds of cattle, they would descry in the centre of the plain an isolated cluster of low hills, crowned with a vast assemblage of temples and palaces, surrounded by their groves and gardens, while the inter-spaces of the hills were filled with the clustering houses which spread around their feet in all the vastness of the greatest city of the world.

They would approach it by the Flaminian Way. For miles outside the city gate the tombs and mausoleums of twenty generations bordered the road, interspersed with the spreading ilex and funereal cypress. Some of these tombs were of considerable size and architectural pretensions, palaces of the dead

each containing the ashes of the members of a noble
family, with those of their freedmen and slaves;
others were of lesser size and sumptuousness, down
to the simple upright head-stone, with its brief epitaph.

As they reached the city, they saw on their left the
Pincian hill, occupied in that day, as in this, by
villas and gardens; from its flank descended the
lofty arches of the aqueduct of Agrippa. On their
right lay the Campus of Agrippa, a public park, with
gardens and porticos, which Augustus had adorned
with a host of statues, taken chiefly from the over-
crowded Capitol. They would soon find themselves
passing, by the Via Lata, through the northern
suburb; the abrupt escarpment of the Capitoline hill
rising before them, and excluding the view of the city.
A winding of the street to right and left again would
take them round the base of the Capitoline, and into
the Forum, where they would be in the very heart
of Rome.

They would see an oblong marble-paved " Place,"
entered by triumphal arches, surrounded by colonnades, lined with temples and basilicas, crowded with
statues. The steep height of the Capitol rose on one
side, crowned with the grand group of buildings which
composed the temple of Jupiter; on the other side,
the Palatine, crowned with the temple of Julius and
the Palace of the Cæsars; all the surrounding heights
sustaining clusters of temples and palaces, surrounded
by groves and gardens; and right in front the colossal
Flavian Amphitheatre. The streets through which
they would pass, in the valleys between these
eminences, were narrow and winding, with lofty brick
houses of many stories, steep gabled, and with over

hanging balconies, making the streets cool and shady under the Italian sun. Forum and streets, in the pleasant evening, would be thronged with all ranks and classes of the gay luxurious city. Gentlemen in embroidered mantles, some strolling under the colonnades, some lounging in groups in the apothecaries' shops, which were then the centres of all the news and all the scandals of the city, as in later times were the barber's shops; ladies in litters of ivory and gold, borne by tall Liburnian slaves trained to walk with regular elastic step, preceded and followed by eunuchs and slave women; the lady herself in silk robe of the lightest texture, rather revealing than veiling her charms, covered with jewels, her hair dyed gold-colour, intermixed with threads of gold and elaborately dressed, her beauty heightened with powder and rouge and darkened eye-lids; citizens and their wives; slaves of all nations and conditions, from the courtly Greek major-domo, or physician, or the staid pedagogue of some great house, down to the negress drudge of some poor craftsman's cabin; gentle and simple, young and old, bond and free, patrician and parasite, gladiator, priest, student, ballad-singer, water-carrier, and slave—all full of life and gaiety, then as now, on a voluptuous summer's evening, in the streets and public places of Rome. Our provincial youths would, probably, on the first day of their arrival, wander through all this magnificence and gaiety, and at length find a lodging high up in one of the tall houses of the Suburra, and settle down for the first evening in their student's chamber, wearied and bewildered, and feeling painfully their own insignificance amidst the crowd and the splendour.

CHAPTER III.

STUDENT LIFE IN ROME.

A.D. 364–367.

THE Emperor Valentinian seems to have revised the educational institutions of the Empire. It was his intention that the arts of rhetoric and grammar should be taught, in the Greek and Latin languages, in the metropolis of every province; and as the size and dignity of the school were usually proportioned to the importance of the city, the academies of Rome and Constantinople claimed a just and singular pre-eminence. Fragments of the edicts of this Emperor for the organization of the school in Constantinople happen to remain, and, no doubt, fairly represent what was the organization of the school of Rome also. That school consisted of thirty-one professors in different branches of learning; viz., one philosopher, and two lawyers; five sophists, and ten grammarians for the Greek; and three orators, and ten grammarians for the Latin tongue; besides seven scribes, or, as they were then styled, antiquarians, whose laborious pens supplied the public library with fair and correct copies of the classic writers. The rule of conduct which was prescribed to the students is the more curious, as it affords the first outlines of the form and discipline of a modern university. It was required that they should bring proper certificates from the magistrates of their native province; their names, professions, and places of abode, were regularly entered in a public register; the studious youth were severely prohibited from wasting their time in feasts or in the theatre; and the term of their education was limited to the age of twenty. The Prefect of the city was empowered to chastise the idle and refractory by stripes or expulsion; and he was directed to make an annual report to the Master of the Offices, that the knowledge and ability of the scholars might be carefully applied to the public service.[1]

The famous Donatus[2] was, at that time, one of the teachers in the schools of Rome, and Jerome and Bonosus had the advantage of his instruction. The regular course of instruction consisted of grammar, *i.e.*, the study of the chief Greek and Latin writers; rhetoric, *i.e.*, the practice of writing and declaiming speeches on all kinds of subjects, which was considered to be the best way to assist the young mind to store up and arrange knowledge, to exercise thought, and to acquire the art of oratory, then so highly

[1] Gibbon, 'Decline and Fall,' ch. xxv.
[2] His most famous work was a system of Latin grammar ('Ars Grammaticus'), which has formed the groundwork of most elementary treatises on the subject from his day to our own times. It was the common school-book of the Middle Ages; insomuch that the word Donat or Donet came to mean an introductory or elementary work in general; *e.g.*, among Bishop Peacocke's works is mentioned, 'The Donat into Christian Religion.' Donatus was the author of Commentaries on the works of Virgil and 'The Plays of Terence,' which have come down to us only in an imperfect form.

esteemed; dialectics, or the art of reasoning and disputation, which added acuteness and readiness to learning and eloquence.

Jerome's natural talent and his industry enabled him to gain a distinguished position in the studies of the Schools; and he acquired a considerable reputation for learning and eloquence. He had, besides, a natural turn for letters; and he bought books, or made copies of them with his own hand, and gradually collected a library. The discipline of the schools of that day, it will be seen, resembled that of the German rather than of the English universities of the present day; the system was professorial, not tutorial; the supervision of the Prefect of the city could be little more than nominal; and the students were practically under no domestic discipline; their own moral principle and discretion were their only guardians amidst the temptations of the capital; and Jerome laments in one of the writings of his maturer years, that his youth and inexperience had succumbed under these temptations.

It is not difficult to picture to ourselves this student life in Rome. The long hours of hard study in the chamber which the two foster-brothers inhabited, in the upper story of one of the tall brick houses; the attendance on professors' lectures, and the declamations and disputations in the schools; the pleasant evenings spent in the Forum, amidst all the wealth and fashion of the capital; the occasional visits to the Flavian Amphitheatre—in spite of the Imperial prohibition—and to the baths of Caracalla or Diocletian, and the gardens of Agrippa. One incident, however, of this student life, which would not, perhaps, have occurred to our imaginations, is suggested by Jerome himself, where he tells us that he used on Sundays, with his companions, to visit the catacombs, and to read the inscriptions on the tombs of the bishops and martyrs. The cessation of the ages of persecution had naturally inclined the present age to look back upon those heroic times of the Church with a sentiment of reverent admiration. Damasus, the archdeacon, had written eulogistic epitaphs on the ancient bishops, and attached them to the loculæ,[1] hitherto marked only by a name. The vistation of the tombs of the martyrs began to be a popular form of piety. This scrap of Jerome's student life enables us to realize the crowd of Roman Christians making a holy-day visit to the suburban cemeteries; defiling, with reverent curiosity, through the narrow subterranean galleries; gazing on the graves which lined their sides, spelling out the brief inscriptions, and guessing at the meaning of the symbols, rudely sculptured upon the slabs which closed them.

It was during Jerome's student life at Rome that Liberius, its bishop, died, and the famous contested election occurred, which placed Damasus in the Episcopal chair.

There were two candidates, the representatives of two parties among the Roman Christians. Damasus represented the party which had rigidly maintained the orthodox faith during the persecution of the Western Church by Constantius, and had rallied round

---

[1] The recesses in the sides of the galleries of the catacombs, in each of which a body was deposited.

Liberius on his return from exile. Ursicinus was the candidate of the laxer party, the party which had surrounded the rival bishop Felix, who had been thrust into the See by Constantius during Liberius's exile. It is said that personal ambition also had its influence in the contest which ensued for the great position of Bishop of Rome; for already, as we have said, it had become a position of wealth and power. The contemporary historian, Ammianus Marcellinus, says: "No wonder that for so magnificent a prize as the Bishopric of Rome, men should contest with the utmost eagerness and obstinacy. To be enriched by the lavish donations of the principal females of the city; to ride, splendidly attired, in a stately chariot; to sit at a profuse, luxuriant, more than imperial table,—these are the rewards of successful ambition."

At the election, which took place in the Church of St. Laurence, the votes were nearly equally divided; Damasus was declared by the presiding officer to be elected, but the partizans of Ursicinus disputed the decision. The two parties came to blows, and the blood of the combatants flowed freely. The party of Damasus remained masters of the field; and Damasus was consecrated by the Bishop of Ostia, to whom tradition assigned the privilege of consecrating the Bishops of Rome.

But the dissension was not thus terminated. Ursicinus denounced the election of his rival as null and void, and of his own authority convoked the people for another election in the Basilica of Sicinius on the Esquiline Mount. The partizans of Damasus, armed with axes swords, and clubs, attempted to

force an entrance into the Basilica, in order to inter-
rupt the proceedings, and disperse the assembly. A
guard of soldiers, sent by the Prefect of the city to
disperse the illegal meeting, marched up in the midst
of the tumult. But the Ursicinians barricaded the
doors of the Basilica, and refused entrance to both
soldiers and crowd. Then the people climbed to the
roof of the building; pulled off the tiles, and flung
them down upon the heads of the assembly within;
the soldiers also assaulted them with arrows and jave-
lins. At last the building was set on fire. Then the
terrified Ursicinians, with the courage of despair,
opened the doors and sallied out; succeeded in
forcing a passage through their besiegers; and dispersed in the neighbouring streets. When the con-
querors entered the Basilica they found the pavement
flooded with gore, and covered with the wounded and
dying; they took out—one account says, 137—another says, 160 corpses. Ursicinus, however, had gone
through the ceremony of an irregular consecration,
and had made his escape.

The whole city was filled with the rioting of the
rival parties. The mob joined the rioters for the
sake of plunder. The military Prefect, Juventius,
withdrew the troops outside the city, whether afraid
of their being overpowered, or to prevent a san-
guinary collision, does not appear. Maximinus, the
Civil Prefect, also withdrew from the city. The
Ursicinians took possession of most of the churches,
and Ursicinus went from one to another, ordaining
a great number of priests and deacons, so as to
surround himself with a clergy; a sufficient indica-

tion that the existing body of the clergy acknowledged
Damasus; which, again, is a strong evidence of the
legitimacy of his claim. At last the commotion
began to subside; Juventius re-entered the city,
and drove out the Ursicinians, who took refuge in
the suburbs, and occupied the cemeteries and
suburban churches, whence they had again to be
driven by force; the Basilica of St. Agnes-without-
the-walls was taken by assault. Meantime, Maximinus
made numerous arrests; examined the accused by
torture; inflicted fines, imprisonment and banishment so lavishly and indiscriminately, as to bring
great odium, not only upon himself, but upon
Damasus and his party. All Italy was moved by
the contest. Ursicinus went from diocese to diocese
seeking support, and demanding a council to decide
between himself and his rival; and carried his
complaints to the Emperor Valentinian. Damasus
similarly addressed himself to the bishops, and to
the Emperor, and appealed to a council.

The Emperor sent Pretextatus, universally respected
for his virtues and ability, though a pagan, to replace
Maximinus as Prefect of Rome, and to restore peace
to the city. But peace was not restored to the
Church till long after, viz., in 381, the Council of
Italy examined into the charges which his enemies
persistently maintained against Damasus, when his
accusers were convicted of falsehood and punished;
Ursicinus was exiled; the few Italian bishops who had
adopted his party were suspended or deposed; the
fair fame of Damasus was cleared, and his lawful
possession of the See of Rome definitely settled.

Thus some three years passed at Rome, and Jerome had arrived at manhood. We next find him at Treves, whether with or without an intervening visit to his paternal home is uncertain. Treves was, at this time, the residence of the Emperor Valentinian, and the head-quarters of his government. It is only conjecture that the talented young man, who had acquired reputation in the schools of Rome, may have been sent here with the view of his entering in some capacity into the service of the State, or taking up the rôle of an advocate before the tribunals. Here he continued his literary pursuits ; he learnt here the native Gallic language ; he tells us that he copied out St. Hilary for his friend Rufinus ; and he seems to have already taken up with ardour the study of theology.

It was while at Treves that that crisis in his religious life occurred which is called his "conversion," and it was at Rome, probably during a subsequent visit, that he received (about A.D. 367) the Baptism which had hitherto been delayed. It was probably also during this second visit that he became connected with the ascetic party among the patrician ladies of Rome, and so entered upon a phase of his life and work which forms one of the most important portions of his subsequent history. In order to understand both this present incident, and the subsequent history, we must describe the development of asceticism in the Western Church at this period, which we shall do more conveniently in a separate chapter.

CHAPTER IV. .

THE first great development of Christian asceticism took place in Egypt, in the time when Athanasius presided over its hundred sees. Antony[1] was not, indeed, the first who adopted a life of solitude and meditation in the desert, but he was the first who acquired a great reputation as an example and teacher of the ascetic life. Multitudes flocked to him, and the deserts began to be peopled with the cells of the solitaries. Pachomius[2] gathered a company of ascetics, and organised them into a society, living apart in an island of the Nile, called Tabenne, and gave them a rule of life. The sister of Pachomius was induced to embrace a similar life in the same neighbourhood, and soon found herself at the head of a large community of nuns, living by her brother's rule. At the same time that Pachomius established his order at Tabenne, Macarius took up his abode in the desert of Scete, a vast solitude near the Libyan frontier; and Ammon established himself on the Nitrian mountain. Each was speedily the centre and head of a great following of hermits; the hermits of Scete living in solitary cells, those of Nitria

---

Died 356.　　　　　　[2] Died 348.

grouped in communities called *Lauræ*. By the end
of the century, the total number of male anchorites
and monks in Egypt was reckoned at 75,000, the
females at 27,000. Hilarion, a pupil of Antony's,
introduced monasticism into Syria, himself occupying,
for 50 years, a cell in the desert near Gaza. Thence
the institution spread into Mesopotamia and Armenia.

In the year 341, Athanasius, compelled to flee
from the persecution of the Arian Eastern Emperor,
Constantius, came to Rome, where he was safe under
the protection of the orthodox Constans. There
came with him two Egyptian anchorites, Ammon and
Isidore, who left the Nitrian desert to attend him in
his exile. The illustrious Bishop was received with
the greatest consideration by the Christians of Rome;
and his companions, the first monks who had been
seen in the west, excited hardly less interest among
them. It was this visit which seems to have introduced into Rome the ascetic spirit which flourished
in the Egyptian Church. Athanasius had written
the life of Antony, though the father of the Egyptian
hermits was still alive. Ammon and Isidore had
known Serapion, the great friend of Antony, and
Macarius, the founder of the communities of Sceté.
They described to their rapt auditors, with the vivid-
ness of eye-witnesses and of partakers in it, that life
of bodily self-mortification and spiritual exaltation
of which Rome had hitherto only heard rumours.
They talked of the monasteries of women ; and of
the Church virgins and widows who, still living in
their families, had devoted their lives to God. They
preached fervently the nobleness and blessedness

of this spiritual life, and incited their hearers to embrace it. The teaching fell on ground prepared to receive it.

The laws of Rome and the customs of its aristocracy gave large wealth to the absolute disposal of the female members of wealthy houses, and left them very independent in the guidance of their own conduct. The patrician ladies of Rome shared in the prevalent spirit of luxury, frivolity, and dissipation. They had vast households of eunuchs and slaves, whom they ruled often with feminine caprice and cruelty. Their toilettes were the most elaborate, costly, and artificial; they painted their faces, and darkened their eyelids after the fashion of the East, and wore the finest textures and the costliest jewels. They rode forth in chariots, or were carried in litters, of gold and ivory, and spent their time at the baths and in the public places; and too often sought in intrigues a zest to the indolent luxury of their lives.

Here, we say, was ground prepared to receive the ascetic teaching of Athanasius and his companions. For it is not only the poor and afflicted and disappointed and ruined who find this world unsatisfactory, and are led to set all their hopes on a higher and future life, and to seek refuge meanwhile in the desert or the cloister. Among the well-born, and wealthy, and luxurious, are always some nobler spirits who find out the vanity of rank and wealth, and experience a satiety of sensuous pleasures; who feel the awful mystery of life, and the craving of an unsatisfied spirit; who learn the lesson of the Scripture, "Let the brother of high degree rejoice in that he is made low, for as the flower of the grass he shall pass away" (James i.); and out of this class also the desert and the cloister have always received a proportion of their inhabitants. The women of the higher class are still more liable to be affected by this spirit than the men ; for the latter have a thousand duties which call them to healthful exertion, or a thousand active pleasures which banish thought; but the unmarried women, limited by the conventions of society within a narrower and more monotonous circle, are left more open to feel the emptiness of the life they lead, and to brood over the great problems of life and death and immortality; and to seek in religion some satisfaction for the yearning of their souls, and some worthy occupation for their days.

It is easy to picture to ourselves the way in which this rise of asceticism would be received in Rome.

We can imagine the indignation of a great patrician, proud of his historic race, which had given consuls to Rome and proconsuls to the provinces, who still lived like a king among his freedmen and slaves, who, albeit rather from pride than belief, still maintained the worship of the ancient gods of Rome —we can imagine his indignation when he found the ladies of his house disregarding the conventions of society, abjuring pride of birth, lavishing their wealth in building churches and giving alms, offending the old manly Roman respect for marriage by embracing virginity, and taking some plebeian priest as the director of their conscience and mode of life.

D

We can imagine the bitterness of a luxurious and courtly clergy when some of their number began to teach, by precept and example, that the clergy ought not to seek presents, and to frequent luxurious tables, and pay their court to fine ladies, to be self-indulgent in their lives and negligent in their duties, but ought to be given to fasting and prayer, to rebuke the fashionable follies and vices of their great patronesses, and to devote themselves to labour among the poor.

It is easy to imagine the sneer with which the average, easy-going Christians of a proud, luxurious age would meet what would seem to them an outbreak of vulgar fanaticism.

And all this old story—fifteen centuries old—has a special interest for us because the history is repeating itself in our time. We modern English people, whose temperament is so wonderfully like that old manly, practical, worldly Roman spirit, suddenly find this ascetic teaching lifting up its voice among us, and a number of our clergy and the ladies of our families strangely attracted towards it. We have to open our eyes to the fact that the conventions of well-to-do society leave our unmarried sisters and daughters in indolent luxury, with no duties to occupy their minds and no career to look forward to ; and we have to make up our minds whether this disposition towards asceticism and Church work is a natural craving for occupation influenced by a false impulse of sentimental antiquarianism, or whether it is really true that the Holy Spirit calls some persons, at least at certain crises in the history of the Church,

to this exceptional devotion, and that all we have to
do is to recognise and regulate it. We have to open
our eyes to the state of religion among clergy and
laity, and to make up our minds whether, in dis-
couraging the ascetic spirit among our clergy, we
should not be crushing the most powerful instrument
for the revival of religion in a careless, worldly state
of the Church, and the most effectual agency for
mission work among the civilized paganisms of the
modern world.

It seems to us impossible to deny the force of the
example of our Lord Jesus Christ, who, for our sakes,
emptied Himself of the glory which He had with His
Father, and became poor, and went about doing good;
and of the Apostles, who gave themselves up to a
life of labours, and dangers, and hardships, and self-
denials; and of the first Christians, who sold their
possessions and goods, and distributed them to them
that had need; and of all those who "went about
in sheepskins and goatskins, destitute, afflicted, tormented, of whom the world was not worthy":—
impossible to say that it is mere fanaticism in those
who follow these examples. God does not call all
men and women to such a course of life, but we
cannot deny that God seems to call some to it, and
that to follow that calling is not fanaticism, but
devotion. The world may still be indignant at the
rebuke conveyed to its worldliness; and the half-
believer may still sneer at the inconceivable fanaticism which really prefers poverty to wealth, humility
to ambition, and self-denial to self-indulgence; but
God forbid that the Church should ever fail to

recognise the excellence of a life of entire self-
devotion !

It is not our business here to discuss these questions, but, in writing the history of Jerome's life,
character, and works, it is impossible to omit them :
he who undertakes to be his biographer must make
up his own mind upon them ; and probably no one
is qualified to be his biographer who has not a strong
sympathy with the general spirit and intention of his
ascetic writings, though with a strong disapprobation
of their extravagances and excesses.

Among the noble ladies of Rome there were some
who willingly listened to the exalted teaching of the
Egyptian ascetics, and from Jerome himself and other
contemporary writers we have details which bring
vividly before us this group of pious women in the
midst of the luxurious society of Rome, and even
brief biographies of several of the most illustrious of
them, and of those who, from time to time, joined
their company during the interval of years from the
visit of Athanasius to the point at which we are arrived
in the history of Jerome.

Foremost among them was Eutropia, the sister of
Constantine, and great-aunt of the reigning emperor.

Abutera and Sperantia were others, whose names
only have been preserved.

Marcella, the only daughter of Albina, a widow of
the most illustrious ancestry, and of great wealth,
Jerome tells us, was the beauty of her time. Married
in early youth, and soon after left a widow, she was
sought in marriage by Cerealis, who was nearly allied

to the Imperial family.   But she had imbibed the
ascetic spirit from the lips of the Egyptian exiles.
She refused a second marriage, in spite of the entreaties of her mother; retired to a villa in the environs
of Rome, surrounded by large gardens; took her
house for a hermitage and her gardens for the
wilderness; and lived there a life of seclusion and
devotion.

Sophronia, another Christian widow, influenced by
Marcella's example, arranged a little cell in her own
house, instead of retiring from the city.

Marcella then, improving on Sophronia's suggestion, consecrated the vast palace of her family on
Mount Aventine to pious reunions, and fitted up an
oratory within it.   This became the centre of a group
of pious ladies, chiefly of the noblest families, widows,
wives, and maidens; some living more or less se-
cluded lives in their own homes; others still living
among their families, and mixing in ordinary society;
but all seeking here support, and sympathy, and
guidance in a devout life.

Asella, a widow, sold her jewels, lived sparingly,
and shared her income with the poor.

Furia, a widow of the noblest family, lived in like
manner.

Fabiola, of equal nobility, young, ardent in her
passions, who had divorced one husband, and married a second, became as ardent in her devotion.

Marcellina and Felicitas are two others, of whom
we know little beyond their names.

Paula, a matron of the most illustrious ancestry,
was already of this pious circle, though it is not till

a later period that her life-long intimacy with Jerome commenced.

We have many indications of the influence exercised by the ladies of Rome in the affairs of the Church at this period.   It was they who, when Constantius visited Rome in 357, walked in procession in their richest attire, through the admiring streets, to ask of the Emperor the return of the banished Bishop Liberius to the city and See, and obtained their petition. It was chiefly their lavish donations and legacies, we learn from Ammianus Marcellinus, which supplied a princely income to the Bishop of Rome.

Melania, a lady with whom Jerome's name became publicly connected during this second visit to Rome, was a young lady of Spanish extraction, but whose family had been settled in Rome for some generations, and was of the highest distinction. Married early, at the age of 23 she lost her husband, and, shortly after, two of her three children.   Instead of giving way to grief, she approached a figure of Christ, with outstretched arms, and a sad smile : " I am the freer to serve Thee, my Lord," she said, " since Thou hast liberated me from these earthly ties." After giving her dead a sumptuous funeral, she announced her intention to depart from Rome ; and in spite of the remonstrances of her family, without making any provision for her surviving child, saying : " God will take care of him better than I," took ship, and sailed for Egypt. This incident excited great interest in Rome. The ascetics praised her sublime faith and devotion ; the pagans complained that these ascetic notions violated the laws of nature, and sapped the bases of society. Jerome's name was mentioned in connection with the incident with reprehension ; probably he had encouraged her flight, or had been among its apologists, or both ; at least, we here see him in his early youth, in those relations with the ascetic Roman ladies which were afterwards renewed, and which entered so largely into the history of his after-life.

CHAPTER V.

JEROME EMBRACES THE ASCETIC LIFE.

A. D. 367--373.

FROM Rome Jerome returned to Aquileia. There he found a knot of enthusiasts, chiefly young men of the higher class of Aquileian society, whose minds were filled with the ascetic ideas which Jerome had lately imbibed. Among them were several of the connections and friends of Jerome,—Paulinian his brother, Bonosus his half-brother, Rufinus, Heliodorus, Chromatius and his brother Eusebius, Jovinus, Innocentius, Nicias, Hylas.

Of this group Rufinus is the most celebrated. We know him as the author of the Ecclesiastical History which has descended to us under his name, and of one or two minor works ; but we know him best by the place which he occupies in the life of Jerome. A friendship sprang up between the two young men, which Jerome spoke of in his writings in such hyperbolical language, and which was made so widely known by those writings, that the two friends were looked upon as another Damon and Pythias. Their early friendship terminated in an acrimonious theological controversy and bitter personal enmity, but we need not anticipate that part of the history. Paulinian has no history of his own; from this period we find him almost constantly beside his brother, playing the part of the *fidus Achates*—the faithful companion and trusted helper, whose life is absorbed in the more vigorous life, whose work is to round off and complete the outlines of the master workman.

Bonosus we already know as the foster-brother of Jerome ; it would seem that at the end of their studentship in Rome he had returned home, while Jerome went to Trèves.

Heliodorus was a young man of noble and wealthy Aquileian family, who had been an officer in the army, but had retired from the service in order to lead a religious life.   He will reappear several times in the subsequent history.   Ultimately he was elected Bishop of Altinum in Venetia.

Chromatius, Eusebius, and Jovinus afterwards entered into holy orders, and in the end became bishops.

Nicias was at present a deacon of the church of Aquileia ; he and Innocentius will shortly reappear in the history.

Hylas was a liberated slave, enfranchised by Melania before her departure from Rome, who had attached himself to Jerome.

The genius and enthusiasm of Jerome, and his recent experience of the ascetic life in the highest ranks of the church at Rome must have given him a great influence among these Aquileian youths, and it was probably his force of character which led them at once to put their ascetic notions into practice.   Some of them, including Rufinus, formed themselves into a religious community in the city itself ; one undertook the hardships of a hermit's life in the neighbouring

Alps ; Bonosus on a desert island off the neighbouring coast. Jerome and his brother retired to their paternal home at Strido, and there gave themselves up to the austerities of an ascetic life.

We may be sure that Jerome proclaimed his ascetic notions with enthusiastic eloquence, and set himself with characteristic vigour to reform everybody and everything about him. His country neighbours seem to have been very unimpressible, and the old Bishop Lupicinus seems to have opposed the novel ideas which his young townsman had brought back from Rome, and to have tried to exercise some control over him. This opposition brought to light the worst side of a great character; opposition enraged him, and this rage sought vent in unscrupulous violence of language. The young ascetic's ideas of the government of the tongue did not prevent him from calling his bishop ignorant, brutal, wicked, unfit for his post, well matched with the flock he ruled, the unskilful pilot of a crazy bark. He gives us already an example of one of the devices by which he habitually sought to throw ridicule on an antagonist, viz. by fastening a nickname on him ; he dubbed his bishop the Hydra.

Disgusted with the opposition he encountered, he and Paulinian quitted their home and buried themselves in a solitary place in the country. But his restless spirit did not long content itself in the solitude ; he returned to Aquileia—to find that most of his friends had equally failed in their first experiment in the ascetic life, and, like himself, had returned to town. But though they had thus failed in their first crude unguided attempt to carry their idea into practice, they had not abandoned the intention ; and when they found themselves together again, they began to talk about visiting Syria or Egypt, the great schools of the ascetic life.

At this crisis an incident occurred which gave definite form to the vague designs floating in their minds. Evagrius, a priest of Antioch, who had been to Rome on the affairs of the Syrian Church, was returning through Aquileia, and his acquaintance determined Jerome and some of his friends to return to Syria with him. Innocentius, Nicias, Heliodorus, and Hylas accompanied Evagrius on his journey by sea. Jerome preferred to travel by land. The two parties met again at Cæsarea in Cappadocia, where they made the acquaintance of the great Basil, its bishop, who, by the recent death of Athanasius, had become the foremost man in the counsels of the orthodox portion of the Church ; and finally they reached Antioch, the great and luxurious capital of the East, at the close of the year 373.

CHAPTER VI.

ANTIOCH AND THE DESERT OF CHALCIS.

A.D. 373–378.

ANTIOCH, built by Seleucus, the great city-builder, for
the capital of his dominions, still ranked as the fourth
of the cities of the world. The population was
composed of four races: the native Syrians; the
Greek colonists; a colony of Jews, whom Seleucus
had attracted to his new capital by the offer of equal
privileges with the Greeks; and, lastly, the Roman
official and military classes, with their belongings.
It had the advantage of a well-chosen site, at the
point where the river Orontes, after flowing north-
wards for 120 miles through the valley of Cœle
Syria, between the two parallel ranges of Lebanon
and anti-Libanus, at length finds an opening between
the Lebanon and the Taurus ranges, and, turning
sharply westward, at the end of twelve miles more
discharges itself into the sea. The harbour of
Seleucia, at the mouth of the river, put the capital
of Asia in easy communication with the Mediterranean, along whose shores lay all the other great
cities of the ancient world. The city lay at the foot
of the pass across Mount Amanus, which formed the
great highway between Asia Minor and Syria; it
occupied the mouth of the valley of Cœle Syria, the
highway to Palestine; and across the great plain of

Antioch, eastward, lay the caravan road by which was carried the trade of the East.

Enlarged and adorned by successive sovereigns, it had grown into a vast and magnificent city. As in many of the Eastern cities built by the Greeks, the backbone of the city was a grand street, four miles long and of considerable width, with a double colonnade, on each side, of marble columns, forming broad double aisles, with, perhaps, a narrow space open to the sky, down the middle of the street. The plan was adapted to an Eastern climate and Eastern habits. The street would form, in fact, a magnificent forum, where, sheltered from the burning Eastern sun, and in the tempered light of the long covered aisles, the groups of citizens and visitors would exhibit all day long that variety of nationality and costume which still makes the bazaars of the Eastern cities so picturesque. From this central street the other transverse streets of the city branched at right angles, running down to the river, which bounded it on the north, and up to the gardens on the slopes of Mount Silpius, whose rugged heights, and torn, craggy summits, bounded it on the south. There were the usual temples, and churches, and basilicas, and theatres, and baths. A temple of Jupiter and a citadel overhung the city from the sides of Silpius. A wall, strengthened at intervals with towers, enclosed the city, running up the steep sides and along the heights of Silpius, forming, in fact, a chain of castles connected by a wall, girding, with their rough strength, the graceful and luxurious Syro-Greek metropolis. The reader will call to mind the special interest of

Antioch in the history of the Christian Church. It was the place where the first Gentile Church was gathered together by the preaching of certain men of Cyprus and Cyrene, who were scattered abroad from Judea upon the persecution that arose about Stephen ; over which Barnabas was sent by the Apostles to preside ; to which Barnabas brought Saul from Tarsus to help him ; which became the great centre of missionary work to Asia Minor and Greece. Here the disciples were first called Christians. Over the Church of Antioch, Ignatius, the disciple of St. John, presided many years, and hence Trajan sent him to his martyrdom in Rome. This Church was one of the three great patriarchal Churches of Christendom, the others being Rome and Alexandria ; its bishop was the chief prelate of the Asiatic portion of the Roman empire. In Rome, we have seen, the pagan temples and their worship were still maintained in splendour, but in the capital of Asia Christianity had long since gained the pre-eminence.[1]

[1] When the Emperor Julian, the apostate, visited the city, and, on the day of the annual festival of Apollo, attended at his temple at Daphne, the lovely suburban village of Antioch, he himself writes :—" I hastened to the sacred grove in the hope that I should there be gratified with the greatest display of your riches and your love of show. I already pictured to myself the festive processions, and saw by anticipation the victims and the holy choirs, the rows of youths attuning their voices in honour of the god, and dressed in garments of dazzling white-ness. But, when I entered the grove, I saw no burning of incense, no wafer-cakes, no victims ! I was at first amazed, though I endeavoured to believe that they were only on the outskirts of the grove, waiting out of compliment to me, as the

Jerome and his companions had come to Antioch at a critical period of the history of its Church ; it was distracted by a threefold schism. Meletius, its bishop, · was orthodox, but tolerant ; his tolerance had led the Arian party to concur in his election to the see, but his orthodoxy soon led to his exile by the Arian Emperor. Then the Arians elected Euzoius, who was formally installed by the Emperor's mandate. But the orthodox refused to recognise Euzoius, and elected Paulinus, who was consecrated by Lucifer of Cagliari and two Occidental bishops. Each of these two rival bishops was recognised by his own party. But after a while Meletius returned from exile and claimed his see. The bishops of the province recognised Meletius as their legitimate patriarch ; but Paulinus refused to give way to him, on the ground that having been elected by a union of Arians with Catholics, he was no better than an Arian bishop ; and part of the Catholic Christians of the city ad-hered to Paulinus, the Arians still recognising only Euzoius.

Evagrius, the most distinguished person of Paulinus's party, had been to Rome and Cæsarea, and other of the great sees on this business, and had obtained for Paulinus the recognition of the Roman See. Jerome and his companions, therefore, found

Pontifex Maximus, for a signal from me for their entrance. When, however, I inquired of the priest, ' What offering does the city intend to bring to-day in honour of the annual festival of the god ?' he answered me, ' I bring from my own house a goose as an offering to Apollo : but the city has prepared nothing for him.' "

themselves, on their introduction into the East, en-
rolled among the partizans of that section of the
Antiochian Church which the Eastern bishops held to
be schismatical. Jerome appears, however, to have
taken no active part in the controversy, but to have
spent his time in diligent study, frequenting the
school of Apollinaris, Bishop of Laodicea, who had a
great reputation as a scholar, a controversialist, and a
subtle expositor of the Christian mysteries.

Jerome had spent some time at Antioch, when a
chance incident again changed his plans. One day
Evagrius took him with him on a visit to the town of
Maronius, of which he was the proprietor, some
thirty miles from Antioch. While there they paid a
visit to an old man called Malchus, who lived, quite
alone, in a wild spot in the neighbourhood. Jerome
was struck with his story, which he afterwards included among his "Lives of the Fathers of the Desert."
The old man, years ago, as he was travelling with a
caravan of merchants through the Valley of the
Orontes, had been captured by a band of nomad
Arabs, who carried him off into the depths of the
desert, and set him to keep their flocks. Lost in
these endless solitudes, and despairing of ever again
seeing friends and country, he was calling upon death
to end his misery, when a woman, his companion in
servitude, spoke to him of God, and restored him to
patience and hope. The two lived near each other
the lives of Christian solitaries, thus turning their
misfortune to religious profit. At last they succeeded
in escaping together. She entered into a convent of
nuns, and he, desiring now no other life than he had

led in the desert, chose out the wild spot where they found him, and there continued his solitary life. The incident rekindled all Jerome's old enthusiasm. He resolved to quit the luxurious capital and retire among the religious of the neighbouring desert of Chalcis.

This desert, situated some fifty miles south-east from Antioch, was tenanted by monks and solitaries. On its western border were several monasteries, whose inmates cultivated the neighbouring soil; still further eastward a crowd of solitaries lived in caves or huts, and raised a scanty subsistence by their labour; while, among the barren mountains and sands of its interior, infested by wild beasts and serpents, a few enthusiasts led a life of terrible endurance, scorched under the Syrian sun in summer, and frozen during the winter nights by the cold winds from the snow-covered mountains.

Jerome's influence over his companions induced them to accompany him to one of the monasteries on the border of the desert. Heliodorus alone declined, and returned to Aquileia. The unhealthiness of the climate, and the hardships of the monastic life, told upon the new comers, and they fell sick. Innocentius died, then Hylas died; Jerome narrowly escaped death. When he recovered he resolved to quit the convent and take up his abode in one of the hermitages, among the solitaries of the desert.

The spiritual charms of this life of solitude are set forth by Jerome himself in a letter which he addressed to Heliodorus—now back in his home in Aquileia, where he had adopted the family of his widowed sister[1]

E

—in which he sought to induce his friend to rejoin him in the desert.

"But what am I saying? Am I again thoughtlessly beseeching you? Away with entreaties and flatteries. Wounded love has a right to be angry. You despised my entreaties; perhaps you will listen to my reproaches. What are you doing in your home, O effeminate soldier! Where are the rampart, and the fosse, and the winter spent in the tented field? Lo, the trumpet sounds from heaven! Lo, the Imperator, all armed, comes amid the clouds, to fight against the world! Lo, a two-edged sword proceeds out of His mouth. He mows down everything which opposes him. And you do not rise from your couch for the battle. You linger in the shade for fear of the sun's heat. Your body is clothed with a tunic instead of a hauberk, your head with a hood instead of a helmet; the rough sword-hilt chafes the hand softened with idleness! Listen to the proclamation of your king— 'He who is not with me is against me, and he who gathers not with me scatters.'

"Remember the day of your enlistment, when buried with Christ in Baptism, you swore to serve Him, to sacrifice everything—even father and mother —to Him. . . . Though your little nephew [1] hang about your neck; though your mother, with rent garments, and head sprinkled with ashes, show you the breasts at which you were nourished; though your father lie stretched across the threshold; go forth over your father's body; go forth, without shedding a tear,

---

[1] Nepotian, of whom we shall hear again.

to join the standard of the cross.   It is piety in such
a matter to be cruel !

"Ah ! I am not insensible to the ties by which you
will plead that you are held back.   My breast, too,
is not of iron, nor my heart of stone ; I was not be-
gotten of the rocks of Caucasus ; the milk I sucked
was not that of Hyrcanian tigresses.[1]   I also have
gone through similar trials.   I picture to myself your
widowed sister hanging about your neck, and trying to
detain you with caresses ; and your old nurse, and
the tutor who had all a father's anxieties over you,
telling you they have not long to live, and begging you
not to leave them till they die ; and your mother, with
wrinkled face and withered bosom, complaining of
your desertion.   The love of God, and the fear of
hell, easily break through such bonds as these !

"You will say the Holy Spirit bids us obey our
parents.   Yes ; but He teaches also that he who loves
them more than Christ, loses his own soul.   .   .   .
'My mother and my brethren,' He says, 'are they
who do the will of my Father which is in heaven.'   If
they believe in Christ, let them encourage you to go
forth and fight in His name ; if they do not believe—
'let the dead bury their dead.'   .   .   .   O desert,
blooming with the flowers of Christ.   O wilderness,
where are shaped the stones of which the city of the
great King is built !   O solitude, where men converse
familiarly with God !   What are you doing among the

[1] Virgil's ' Æneid,' bk. iv.   Dido says to Æneas :—
   " No—'twas from Caucasus you sprung,
     And tigers nursed you with their young."
                  —Connington's translation, p. 116.

worldly, O Heliodorus, you who are greater than all
the world? How long shall the cover of roofs weigh
you down ; how long shall the prison of the smoking
city confine you?

"Do you fear poverty? But Christ calls the poor
blessed. Are you frightened at the prospect of
labour? But no athlete is crowned without sweat.
Are you thinking about daily food? But faith fears
not hunger. Do you dread to lay your fasting body
on the bare ground? But Christ lies beside you.
Do the tangled locks of a neglected toilet shock you?
But your head is Christ. Your skin will grow rough
and discoloured without the accustomed bath, but he
who is once washed by Christ needs not to wash
again.[1] And, in fine, listen to the Apostle, who
answers all your objections, ' The sufferings of this
present world are not worthy to be compared with
the coming glory which shall be revealed in us.'[2]
You are too luxurious, my brother, if you wish both
to enjoy yourself here with the world and afterwards
to reign with Christ. Does the infinite vastness of
the wilderness terrify you? Walk in spirit through
the land of Paradise, and while your thoughts are
there, you will not be in the desert."[3]

In the stern exhortation to Heliodorus to break
all natural ties, we recognise the spirit which might
have prompted or defended the flight of Melania,
which did in after years encourage Paula to a like act
of stoicism.

In this beautiful—though a little rhetorical—de-

John xiii. [2] Romans viii. 18. [3] Ep. v. ad Heliodorum.

scription of the spiritual joys of the desert, we see one side of the solitary life. In another letter (ad Eustochium, Ep. xviii) Jerome exhibits, on the other hand, his experience of the hardships of the life, and the temptations of · solitude, with a frankness which lays bare his very soul to our gaze: "Ah! how often, when I dwelt in the desert, have I, in the midst of that vast solitude which surrounded the dreadful cell, fancied myself among all the delights of Rome. I sat alone because my soul was filled with bitterness. My shapeless limbs were clad in a frightful sack, my squalid skin had taken the hue of an Ethiop's flesh. I spent whole days shedding tears and breathing sighs, and when, in spite of myself, I was overcome with sleep, I let fall, upon the naked earth, a body so emaciated that the bones scarce held together. I will say nothing of my food or drink, even the sick had nothing but cold water, and to eat anything cooked was luxury. Yet I—who for fear of hell, had condemned myself to such a dungeon, the companion of scorpions and wild beasts—I often imagined myself in the midst of girls dancing. My face was pallid with fasting, and yet my soul glowed with desire in my cold body. My flesh had not waited for the destruction of the whole man, it was dead already, and yet the fires of the passions boiled up within me. Thus, destitute of all help, I cast myself at the feet of Jesus, I bathed them with my tears, I wiped them with my hair. I tried to conquer this rebellious flesh by a week of fasting. I often passed the night and day in crying, and beating my breast, and ceased not till,

God making Himself heard, peace came back to me.
Then I feared to return to my cell as if it had known
my thoughts, and full of anger and severity against
myself I plunged alone into the desert. When I saw
some nook of the valleys, some wild spot in the
mountains, some precipice among the rocks, there I
made the place of my prayers, and the prison of my
miserable body ; and, as God Himself is my witness,
sometimes after having shed floods of tears, after
having for a long time lifted my eyes to heaven, I
believed myself transported into the midst of the
choirs of angels ; and, filled with confidence and joy,
I sang, ' We will run after thee, for the odour of thy
perfumes.' "[1]

These, however, were only occasional experiences.
The ordinary life Jerome led in his hermitage was of
a quiet and regular kind. He had brought his
library with him into the desert, and occupied a great
part of his time in study. His studies were carried
on with energy and method. Evagrius, who visited
him from time to time, brought him books, and supplied him with scribes, who copied books for him, or
wrote at his dictation. Neighbouring monks and
solitaries occasionally visited him to discuss questions
of scholarship or points of theology with him. He
also kept up a correspondence with his numerous
friends, of which the letter to Heliodorus above
quoted, may be taken for an example.

After awhile, his usual studies were interdicted by
a dream or vision, which pronounced them incon-

---

[1] Song of Solomon, i. 3, 4.

sistent with his spiritual vocation.   Thus he himself relates the story: " When years ago I had torn myself from home and parents, sister and friends, for the kingdom of heaven's sake, and had taken my journey for Jerusalem,[1] I could not part with the books which I had collected at Rome with very great care and labour.   And so, unhappy man that I was, I followed up my fasting by reading Cicero ; after a night of watching, after shedding tears, which the remembrance of my past sins drew from my inmost soul, I took up Plautus.   If sometimes, coming to myself, I began to read the prophets, their inartistic style repelled me.   When my blinded eyes could not see the light, I thought the fault was in the sun, not in my eyes.   While the old serpent thus deceived me, about the middle of Lent a fever seized me, and so reduced my strength that my life scarce cleaved to my bones. They began to prepare for my funeral.   My whole body was growing cold, only a little vital warmth remained in my breast ; when suddenly I was caught up in spirit, and brought before the tribunal of the Judge.   So great was the glory of his presence, and such the brilliancy of the purity of those who surrounded Him, that I cast myself to the earth, and did not dare to raise my eyes.   Being asked who I was, I answered that I was a Christian.   'Thou liest,' said the Judge, 'thou art a Ciceronian, and not a Christian, for where thy treasure is, there is thy heart also.'   Thereupon, I was silent.   He ordered me to be beaten, but I was tormented more by remorse of

---

[1] That being his intended destination when he started.

conscience than by the blows, I said to myself 'Who shall give thee thanks in hell?' Then I cried, with tears, 'Have mercy upon me, O Lord, have mercy upon me.' My cry was heard above the sound of the blows. Then they who stood by, gliding to the knees of the Judge, prayed Him to have mercy on my youth, and He gave me time for repentance, on pain of more severe punishment if I should read pagan books in the future. I, who in such a strait, would have promised even greater things, made oath, and declared by His sacred Name, 'O Lord, if ever I henceforth possess profane books or read them, let me be treated as if I had denied Thee.' After this oath, they let me go, and I returned to the world. To the wonder of all who stood by, I opened my eyes, shedding such a shower of tears, that my grief would make even the incredulous believe in my vision. And this was not mere sleep, or a vain dream, such as often deludes us. The tribunal before which I lay is witness, that awful sentence which I feared is witness, so may I never come into a like judgment. I protest that my shoulders were livid, that I felt the blows after I awoke, and thenceforward I studied divine things with greater ardour than ever I had studied the things of the world." [1]

It was probably one consequence of this new phase of mind that he set himself as a task to learn Hebrew. A converted Jew happened to be living in one of the neighbouring monasteries as a monk, and Jerome availed himself of his help as a tutor. He complained bitterly of the difficulty and distasteful-

[1] Epistle xviii. ad Eustochium, § 30.

ness of the study, but he thus laid the foundation of that knowledge of the original language, which bore such valuable fruits afterwards in his version of the Old Testament, and his commentaries upon it.

Three years thus passed away.   Meantime, the distractions of the Church of Antioch had been growing more complicated.   Meletius tried to mitigate the schism by some arrangement with Paulinus. First, Meletius proposed to Paulinus that they should reunite their followers—who were perfectly agreed on all points, except on the one whom they should recognise as their bishop—and should exercise a joint episcopate over the Catholic flock. This Paulinus refused, on the old ground that the Arians had concurred in Meletius's election, and that he would not soil himself with any contact with heresy.   Then Meletius proposed to prevent at least, the perpetuation of the schism by an agreement between the two parties, that on the death of either of the two bishops, their flocks should reunite under the rule of the survivor.   To this Paulinus and his party agreed; Meletius was the older man, and it offered them the prospect of ultimate triumph.   An assembly of the clergy of the two parties was held, they solemnly accepted the arrangement, and six on each side swore on behalf of themselves and their brethren to observe it.   Flavian, the most distinguished of the Meletian clergy, was the first to take the oath; and of him and this oath we shall hear again.

But now the Syrian bishops, who had supported

the claims of Meletius, refused to concur in this agreement, and accused Meletius of betraying them. The succession of Paulinus to the See of Antioch would make him the ecclesiastical ruler of the Bishops of Asia. But he was not one of them. The Christianity of the East and that of the West formed two very distinct "schools" in the Church, and Paulinus, by his antecedents, and sympathies, and alliances, belonged to the Western school. It was not merely a spirit of personal antagonism to Paulinus, but a jealousy of the Roman Church—which had promoted the consecration and supported the pretensions of Paulinus—which made the Syrian bishops decline to recognise Paulinus as their patriarch should he survive Meletius. The division was thus further complicated, and new bitterness introduced into the quarrel.

Besides this fourfold schism, two distinct doctrinal controversies agitated the Syrian Church at the same time.

A dispute, which turned on the ambiguous use of a theological expression, had arisen in the Syrian Church. The words *ousia* and *hypostasis* had, in the beginning of the Arian controversy, been used by the Orientals as equivalent ; both had been translated by the Latin word *substantia*, and had been understood by the Latins as signifying the *nature* of God ; but a distinction had been introduced in the East, and had been adopted by Meletius and the Syrian bishops, by which *ousia* continued to be used to denote the *nature* or essence of God, while *hypostasis* was taken to express that which we are accustomed to denote by the word *person*.   The Latins, hearing that three *hypostases* were maintained by Meletius, took alarm, as if three *substances* were held, implying a division of the divine substance; while the Easterns insisted on the necessity of using the word *hypostasis* in the new sense given to it, considering that the use of the Greek word *prosopon*, which answered to the Latin *persona*, savoured of Sabellianism, as expressing rather three *manifestations* of the one Godhead, than that distinction which is asserted in the Catholic doctrine.[1]

Meletius and his party, and the Syrian Church generally, adopted the new nomenclature of three *hypostases* in one *ousia*.   Paulinus and his party maintained, with the African and Western Churches that the new nomenclature was unnecessary and full of danger, and refused to adopt it.[2]

Moreover, a new heresy had broken out in the Syrian Church.   The brilliant Bishop of Laodicea (Apollinaris), once regarded as one of the most redoubtable champions of orthodoxy, had now himself put forth a new theory as to the union of the two natures in Christ, which, to say the least, was plainly unorthodox.

Adopting the Platonic analysis of human nature into body, animal or vital soul, and intellectual or rational soul, he maintained that the divine Logos. in his incarnation, had taken only the body and vital soul, and that the Logos supplied the place of the rational soul, thus contravening the doctrine of the

[1] Robertson's 'Hist. of the Christian Church.'
[2] It was ultimately adopted, however, by the whole Church.

true and perfect humanity of Christ. The Apollinarians rent the Church of Antioch with another schism, and elected Vitalis as their Bishop.

These controversies greatly excited the whole Syrian Church, and were taken up with vehemence by the monks and solitaries of the desert.

As a member of the Western Church, and a friend of Paulinus, Jerome found himself an object of suspicion among his neighbours. He tried to keep free of the local parties, declaring that he had nothing to do with either Vitalis, or Meletius, or Paulinus. (Non novi Vitalem, respuo Meletium, ignoro Paulinum [1]) that he simply adhered to the Church of his baptism, and that he was in communion with all who were in communion with Rome. (Si quis cathedræ Petri jungitur meus est.) When he declined to adopt the new phraseology of three *hypostases*, they accused him of heresy; he replied that they could not condemn him as a heretic without condemning the Western and African Churches. He wrote to Marcus: [2] "You clearly think that I am a man of great eloquence, who am going about the Churches preaching in Syrian or in Greek, seducing the people, and creating a schism. All I ask," he says, " is to be allowed to hold my tongue, and to be let alone. If I am a heretic, what is that to you; let me alone, and there is an end of the matter."

At length he and his friends resolved to quit the desert. They left at once. He, on account of his ill-health remained, until the spring made travelling less

[1] Ep. v. ad Damasum.
[2] Epistle xv. ad Marcum Presbyterum.

difficult; then he also turned his back on the desert and its inhabitants, having, no doubt, in his mind the verse of Virgil which he had quoted in his letter to Marcus :—

Quid genus hoc hominum ; quæve hunc tam barbara morem
. Permittit patria ? Hospitio prohibemur arenæ.

What race of mankind is this ? What is the barbarous country which permits such customs ? We are refused the hospitality even of a little sand.[1]

Returning to Antioch Jerome continued to study and to write. It was now he wrote his ' Chronicle,' published a little later at Constantinople ; ' A Dialogue against the Luciferians,' a piece of theological controversy ; ' A Life of Paul the Hermit,' a companion of Antony, the life of the latter having already been written by Athanasius ; and some other of his earliest works. His reputation as a scholar and a writer was established in the Eastern Church. Paulinus was anxious to attach him to himself, and pressed the priesthood upon him.

There was a fashion at that time of forcing the priesthood or the episcopate upon men who seemed to the heads of the Church fit, though unwilling, and Paulinus seems to have practised some of this coercion upon Jerome ; for at the time of his ordination he thus addressed the bishop : " My father, I have not asked the priesthood, and if, in conferring it upon me, you do not take away the character of monk, I do not object ; you must be responsible for the opinion you have formed of me ; but if, under the

[1] Epistle xv. ad Marcum Presbyterum.

pretext of the priesthood, you propose to take away my liberty to return to a solitary life, and to plunge me again into the world which I have renounced, you deceive yourself; for to me this liberty is the sovereign good. " Now, do what you will; my new condition will be no loss, if it be no gain, to the Church."[1] It is said that he never once, even in cases of pressing necessity, exercised the office thus thrust upon him.

It is probable that at this period he made a journey to Palestine, and visited the Holy Places; and that it was on the conclusion of this journey he took up his abode in Constantinople, where he spent the next three years of his unsettled life.

[1] Ep. xxxviii.

CHAPTER VII.

NEW ROME.

A.D. 379–382.

THE reader will not fail to observe how the course ot our narrative carries us to all the great cities of the Roman world ; already to Rome and Antioch, now to Constantinople, hereafter to Alexandria. Since our object is not only to give a life of Jerome, but also a general view of the Church in the period in which he lived, we take advantage of these opportunities for sketching the condition of things in those cities which were the capitals of Christendom as well as of the Roman Empire.

The Sovereigns of the Empire had ceased to reside at Rome for many years,[1] before Constantine the Great resolved to found a new capital. His choice of a site has ever since commanded the approval of the statesman and the soldier for its political, military, and commercial advantages, and the admiration of all who have had the good fortune to visit it for its exceeding beauty. It is at this moment[2] the great prize for whose possession two nations are lavishing their blood and treasure, while the rest of the nations look on in arms, resolved to have a voice in the ultimate decision of a question of such vast political im

---

[1] See p. 5.   [2] (Jan., 1878.)

portance to the whole civilized world. The city of
Constantine was built on seven hills which diversify
the surface of a triangular spur of land between the Sea
of Marmora and the crescent-shaped arm of the
Bosphorus called the Golden Horn. Its erection
was urged forward with all the power and wealth at
the command of the energetic Master of the World.
A description of the city, of the period of which we
are writing, gives us some idea of its magnificence by
enumerating among its buildings " a capitol, a school
of learning, a circus, two theatres, eight public, and
one hundred and fifty-three private baths, fifty-two
porticoes, five granaries, eight great aqueducts or re-
servoirs of water, four spacious halls for the meetings
of the senate or courts of justice, fourteen churches,
fourteen palaces, and four thousand three hundred
and eighty-eight houses, which, for their size or
beauty, deserved to be distinguished from the multitude of plebeian habitations.[1] " The whole city was
strongly fortified ; on the two sides defended by the
sea a lofty, and massive wall, thickly studded with
towers, was considered sufficient ; on the land side
was a second line of wall, with towers at very short
intervals, with deep moats ; and still a third 'avant
mure,' with its moat, made a triple line of fortifica-
tion. The city was enriched with statues and works
of art culled from the greatest works of the old Greek
artists. A population was attracted by grants of
palaces and estates to the great ; privileges and
the prospect of wealth from the expenditure of the

---

[1] Gibbon's ' Decline and Fall.'

Court and the pursuit of commerce were enough to create a middle class; and vast largesses, imitated from the daily doles which were distributed among the citizens of Old Rome, helped to fill New Rome with a numerous population. In front of the palace the founder erected a colossal statue of himself, bearing in his hand the laurel-crowned monogram of Christ, which was also impressed on the standards of the army and the coinage of the Empire, and proclaimed that the new capital was the crowning work of the policy which had given a new constitution and a new religion to the Empire.

When the town of Byzantium was a little town in the civil province of Heraclea, its Church had been a subordinate Church, subject to the Archbishop of the metropolis; but the ecclesiastical constitution, which had originally followed the civil territorial divisions, readily adapted itself to the occasional modifications made in the political arrangements, and the dignity of the new capital at once secured for its Church an independent position, and for its bishop the titular rank of a metropolitan. Wealth naturally accrued to the Bishop of New Rome, and his position at the residence of the Emperor naturally gave him great influence and high consideration. But there was always this difference between his position and that of the other great prelates of the Church, that this very position at the capital prevented him from exercising so independent an authority as the others. At this moment the Bishop of Alexandria was the most powerful man in Egypt, and the Bishop of Rome within a very few years had no rival in Rome; but

F

the Bishop of Constantinople was only a great eccle
siastical official among many great civil and military
officials who surrounded the throne of the Emperor ot
the East.

It was remarkable that while Constans and Valentinian, who so long ruled the West, were orthodox,
their brothers, Constantius and Valens, who ruled the
East, were Arians. So that, while the Church of the
West had enjoyed peace, except during the short
period of the sole rule of Constantius, the Church of
the East had undergone a long period of conflict and
persecution. For forty years past the see of Constantinople had been filled by a succession of Arian bishops.

Valentinian died in 375 A.D., and was succeeded
by his son Gratian at the age of 16. In August, 378,
Valens perished in the disastrous battle against the
invading Goths at Adrianople. The young Emperor,
Gratian, summoned Theodosius to assist him to defend
the State, and committed to him the Empire of
the East. Theodosius was orthodox, and with his
accession a brighter prospect dawned for the Churches
of the East.

Basil of Cæsarea, who had long been the leader of
the orthodox party in the East, induced Gregory of
Nazianzum to undertake a mission to the capital, and
to endeavour to rally the depressed and scattered
orthodox Christians of the imperial city. Basil and
Gregory had been youths together in the schools of
the Cappadocian Cæsarea, and their acquaintance
had ripened into intimate friendship during the years
in which they completed their education at Athens.
Basil, after some years of travel, founded monasteries

in the desert of Pontus, and Gregory withdrew from the world with him. When Basil was elected Archbishop of Cæsarea, he forced the episcopate upon Gregory, who refused to take possession of his see of Sasima, but was persuaded to assist his aged father in the administration of his see of Nazianzum. On his father's death he withdrew again into retirement. He was of gentle, unworldly, and retiring disposition, but had a great reputation for piety, learning, and eloquence.

The task which, at Basil's request, he undertook was an arduous one. Demophilus, an Arian, was the bishop, the Arians had possession of the whole Church organization of Constantinople, the orthodox had not a single church or congregation, and Gregory was obliged to gather his little flock together in a private house. At the outset he had to encounter much opposition; his church was invaded by night, and profaned; he was brought before the magistrates as a disturber of the peace; he was assaulted in the streets: but he quietly persevered, and his saintly character and his eloquence gradually made a great impression. It was just at this time, viz., in the year 379, that Jerome took up his abode in Constantinople. He adhered, of course, to the party of Gregory; his scholarship and his energy could not fail to make him a person of some importance among the growing orthodox party; and he acknowledges, in after years, the friendship of Gregory, and the advantages he derived from intercourse with him and the other learned men with whom he then associated.

In the following year, A.D. 380, Theodosius found

leisure to visit the capital, and among other things to regulate the affairs of its Church. Demophilus and his clergy, refusing to accept the orthodox creed, were ejected from their offices. The Catholics demanded Gregory for their new bishop, and on his refusal the people, according to the custom of the time already mentioned, used a friendly violence, and installed him by force in the episcopal throne. Gregory accepted the position provisionally, but made his final acceptance conditional on his acknowledgment by his brother prelates at the approaching Council; for Theodosius had summoned a Council of the Eastern bishops to meet at the Capitol in the following year, 381, to settle the many questions of doctrine and discipline which distracted the Churches of the East.

The few months which intervened, gave opportunity to set up a rival claimant. The See of Alexandria was jealous of the new see which eclipsed her own dignity. There was, indeed, at the moment, an interregnum in the Egyptian Church; but Peter the Archdeacon cared for its interests. The annual Egyptian fleet, bearing the harvests of the Delta for the sustentation of the capital, sailed in the autumn; Peter sent with it one Maximus, a creature of his own, and several Egyptian bishops, and arranged with the chiefs of the flotilla to support the intrigue. Arrived at Constantinople, they organized an agitation against Gregory. One night the conspirators obtained entrance to the principal church, the Egyptian bishops consecrated Maximus, and enthroned him as Bishop of Constantinople.

The Council met in the middle of May, A.D. 381,

it consisted entirely of Eastern bishops. Meletius, whose position as rightful Bishop of Antioch had recently been decided by an Imperial Commission, presided; the Council recognised his claim to the see, and declared the compact between him and Paulinus null and void. The agitation of the stormy scenes which disturbed the opening sittings of the Council was too great for the aged bishop; he sickened and died : but not before the claim of Gregory to the See of Constantinople had been formally recognised by the Council.

On the death of Meletius, and on the rescinding of the compact by which Paulinus was to be acknowledged as his successor, Flavian returned at once to Antioch, and was elected by the party of Meletius as his successor in the see. Gregory succeeded to the presidency of the Council, and the business proceeded. Then Timothy, newly elected to the See of Alexandria, arrived with a great train, and fresh difficulties arose. Timothy protested against the opening of the Council in his absence; he supported the claim of Maximus against Gregory, and demanded the reconsideration of the question. Gregory, always anxious for peace, resigned his pretentions to the see; but then the Council rejected Maximus ; and the progress of events was arrested until a new election could be made. The choice was referred to the Emperor, who nominated a nobleman of the name of Nectarius. According to the evil custom of the time, Nectarius's baptism had been delayed, and at the time of his election he was only a catechumen. He was baptized, consecrated, enthroned, and at once took his seat as president of the Council, wearing his episcopal robes over the white dress of the newly baptized. The Council then proceeded with its business. It revised and enlarged the Nicene Creed so as to condemn the Macedonian heresy on the divinity of the Holy Ghost; it condemned the Apollinarian heresy described above;[1] it settled the disputed disciplinary questions about the sees of Constantinople, Antioch, Alexandria, Jerusalem; and recognised the dignity of the see of the new capital of the Empire by assigning to the Bishop of New Rome, a position equal in rank with the three great ancient patriarchates, and next in precedence after the See of ancient Rome.

Before the Council was concluded, a synodical letter of the Western bishops arrived, announcing their intention to hold a general council of the Church at Rome in the following year, and a rescript from the Emperor Gratian inviting the attendance of the Eastern bishops. It is probable that Ambrose, the great Bishop of Milan, who had great influence over the young Emperor, concurred in the planning of this council, though, when the time came, a fit of illness prevented him from taking any part in its proceedings.

The history of this Roman Council is very curious and very important in its bearing upon the question of the subsequent pretensions of the Roman See.

It was an attempt to set up a rival Council to that which had been summoned to meet at Constantinople. It put forth, as a reason for its convocation,

that there were rival claimants to all the great sees of
the East—Constantinople, Alexandria, Antioch, and
Jerusalem—and it proposed to pronounce judgment
upon all these rival claims. The letter summoning
the council shadowed forth the judgment which the
See of Rome was prepared to pronounce. In the
case of Constantinople, it assumed that Maximus,
whose clandestine and irregular intrusion into the See
of Constantinople by a handful of Egyptian bishops
had been at once repudiated by the Church of Constantinople, was the legitimate possessor of the see,
and that the election of Nectarius was clearly null.
Nectarius, it said, could only have been nominated in
violation of all ecclesiastical rules, and he was not
even baptized at the time of his election ! In the
case of Antioch, it upheld Paulinus, as the only
Catholic bishop since the death of Meletius ; Flavian,
it declared, was only a false bishop, an intruder, a
perjurer, who held the see contrary to his own solemn
engagements. In the case of Jerusalem, it upheld
the claims of Hilarius, who had been elected during
the exile of the saintly Cyril, against Cyril, who had
since returned to his see, on the ground that Cyril was
despotic and tyrannical ; that he had been scandalously
insubordinate to his metropolitan, who was an Arian ;
had by intrigues procured the election of his own
nephew to the See of Cæsarea ; and had sold an embroidered robe given by Constantine to his Church,
which had come into the hands of a comedian, who
used it on the stage. In the case of Alexandria, the
letter maintained the claims of Timothy in the disputed election to that see. The claim to settle in a

Roman Council the affairs of all the great sees of Christendom was so large a claim, that the letter put forth an apology for it, "We do not claim the prerogative of judgment on these questions, but we claim a part, a simple part, in decisions which concern the whole Church."

The Eastern bishops assembled at Constantinople had, meantime, settled all the questions thus enumerated. The Eastern bishops were very indignant at this attempt to bring them to Rome for the settlement of the affairs of the East, and their reply to the bishops of the West is a fine piece of irony. They begin by reciting the sufferings of the oriental Churches during the Arian persecutions, and contrasting it with the peace which the West had enjoyed since the time of Constantine. They excuse themselves from undertaking the long and dangerous journey to Rome, and leaving their sees which so much needed their fostering care; yet in evidence of the spirit of charity, which animates them, they say they have deputed three of their number to present to the assembled fathers at Rome the results of the Council of Constantinople, and to make their excuses for non-attendance at Rome; and the three representatives thus sent were three bishops of insignificant sees, and themselves unknown men. As to the regulation of the affairs of the metropolitan sees of the East, which had excited so keen an anxiety in the breasts of the prelates of the West, the Council of Constantinople simply, without any argument or explanation, notifies its decisions to the Council of Rome. It declares that the prelates, whose claims to the several sees had been thus decided, merit the respect of the Church, and the congratulations of the bishops of the West. The prelates thus commended were, except in the case of Alexandria, precisely those against whose claims the Roman See had rashly declared itself. The ceremonious announcements contrast forcibly with the statements of the Roman letter : " We have," say the oriental fathers, " instituted as bishop of the most illustrious Church of Constantinople, the very holy and very reverend Nectarius, with unanimous consent, in the presence of the most religious Emperor Theodosius, and in conformity with the suffrages of the clergy, and of the whole city." . . . "We have equally taken care, for the necessities of the Church of Antioch, that ancient and truly apostolic city, where the believers were first called Christians. The most holy and most reverend Flavian, having been elected and appointed by the unanimous concurrence of the city, of his clergy, and of the bishops of the diocese of the East, we have, with one voice, ratified his appointment." . . . " In the Church of Jerusalem, ' that mother of all churches,' the Council has maintained as its bishop, ' the most venerable Cyril, its lawful bishop, a courageous confessor of the Catholic faith, proved in combats against the perfidious Arians, and by various banishments and imprisonments.' " . . . . Finally, the Council exhorts the Roman prelates to put aside all respect of persons in their judgment upon the settlement of affairs, and to have regard only to the welfare of the Church. " If all the world," it says, ' would be guided by this wholesome rule, the body of the Church would become like that of Christ Himself, whole and entire."

The Emperor, Theodosius, gave a more brief and peremptory refusal to the request that he would command the attendance of the Eastern bishops at this Roman Council. To ask the Eastern bishops to come to Rome for the settlement of their affairs, he said, was absurd, was offensive; the orientals should not come! The right of each Church to regulate its own affairs, and to elect its chiefs, was set forth in the canons of the Church; and to deny it, or question it, was to create a public danger. He reproached the Western prelates with having been duped by Maximus, and with the rancorous spirit they nourished against the Churches of the East.

The whole incident is characteristic of the relations of the Churches at this period. The Church of Rome for the first century or more had been a Greek mission in the midst of the Latin race. The Greek world—and Alexandria, Antioch, and Constantinople were Greek—from the height of their subtle polished intellect still looked down upon the West as vigorous, but rude and unpolished. Of all the great thinkers, and writers, and rulers of Christendom, not one had yet been contributed by the Italian Church; not a single man of note had yet occupied the See of Rome. If Liberius occupies some space in the history of the Church, it is his failure under the persecution of the Arian Emperor, Valens, it is his consent to sign the ambiguous creed of Sirmium, which give him his place in history. Damasus was the first Roman bishop who made any considerable mark on the history of the Church. With his episcopate the ambitious spirit of the Roman Church is clearly marked. Basil had already had occasion to say, " I hate the pride of that (Roman) Church." The letter of invitation to this Roman Council exhibits the Roman craving to take into its hands the discipline of the whole Church; the reply of the Council of Constantinople marks the contempt with which these pretensions were at present regarded. It is the fine irony of a consciously superior intellect foiling the crude aggressiveness of a powerful but clumsy assailant.

The Roman Council met, and was largely attended by the Western bishops, but only two of the Eastern bishops obeyed their summons : Paulinus, of Antioch, whose Western connections we have already seen, who came to plead his own claims to the See of Antioch, with good reason to anticipate that they would be recognised at Rome ; and Epiphanius, Archbishop of Salamis (Cyprus), who was a friend of Paulinus, and like him, in relations with Rome and Alexandria, who came not only to support his friend, but especially to plead for the condemnation of the Apollinarian heresy. Jerome, though he had not been summoned to the council, had agreed with his friend and bishop, Paulinus, to accompany him thither.

The noble Roman Christians opened their houses to receive the fathers of the Church as honoured guests during the sitting of the Council. We are not surprised to find Jerome received as the guest of Marcella, in her palace on the Aventine, the head-quarters of

the ascetic party in Rome.   We are, however, surprised to find him, who had not even received a formal
invitation to attend the Council, and who must have
been unknown to the great body of these Western
bishops, nominated by Damasus and accepted by
the rest, for the responsible and honourable position
of Secretary of the Council.

The Roman Council accepted the decision of the
Council of Constántinople in the cases of Nectarius
and Cyril, but it maintained the claims of Paulinus,
whose cause the Western bishops had all along
supported, and who had now moreover deserved
their favour by coming to submit his case to their
decision.   They proceeded to consider the case of
the Apollinarians.   Damasus had excluded them in
375 from communion with the Roman Church, and
they had appealed from his sentence to a council ;
they now appeared in support of their appeal by
some of their most able representatives, by whose
dialectic skill they hoped that they might obtain a
favourable verdict from the Western bishops, whose
theological acumen and controversial skill were not
highly esteemed in the East.   But Epiphanius had
come to the Roman Council to oppose them.   They
could hardly have had a more formidable opponent.
He had made a special study of the heresies of the
Church, and had published a great work called
"Panarium," in which he had analysed, and classified,
and confuted them to the number of 100 ; his con-
temporaries jestingly accused him of having given
rise to several by his definition and publication of
them.   The Apollinarian advocates could not hold

their ground against him ; they were driven from one position to another, until at last they acknowledged themselves conquered in argument, and requested terms of reconciliation. It was intrusted to the Secretary of the Council to draw up the formulary of orthodox belief, which they should sign as the condition of their restoration to Catholic communion. The Apollinarians subsequently accused him of having fraudulently altered the document after it had received their signatures. There does not appear to have been any truth in the charge, but it afforded a weapon to Jerome's enemies in after years.

The Council failed to answer the expectations of those who had convoked it. The Council of Constantinople was gradually received everywhere as the second great Ecumenical Council, while its Roman rival shrunk to the dimensions of a local synod of no special importance ; but it had brought Jerome into close relations with the Bishop of Rome, and put him prominently before the eyes of the Western Church.

CHAPTER VIII.

THE SECRETARY OF THE ROMAN SEE.

A.D. 382–385.

THE Council concluded, and the bishops dispersed to their sees; but Damasus had discovered the abilities of Jerome, and retained him in Rome in the capacity of secretary of the Roman See.

From the letters of Damasus, as well as of Jerome, it is manifest that the aged bishop had conceived a very high opinion of his young secretary's learning and judgment. In the official correspondence of the see, Jerome was not merely an amanuensis who wrote what the bishop dictated, he was rather the real author of the state papers which the bishop approved and signed. He himself says of their relations, that "Damasus was his mouth." The bishop had also enough of learning himself, and love of learning, to appreciate the greater learning of his secretary, and to avail himself of it. He consulted Jerome as to his own reading, read Jerome's books and urged him to write others, and consulted him on points of Scriptural criticism and exegesis.

These Scriptural conferences led at length to very important results. The bishop urged Jerome to undertake a thorough revision of the Latin version of the Gospels; and this was the first step towards the ultimate retranslation of the Scriptures from the original languages into Latin, on which the fame of Jerome rests.

The history of the earliest Latin version of the Bible is lost in complete obscurity; all that can be affirmed with certainty is, that it was made in Africa. During the first two centuries, the Church of Rome was essentially Greek ; the Roman bishops of that period bear Greek names; the earliest Roman Liturgy was Greek ; the few extant remains of the Christian literature of Rome are Greek. The same remark holds true of Gaul. But in North Africa[1] Carthage, its capital, and probably most of its towns, had inherited, from the conquests of Scipio, the Roman language and civilization ; the Church of North Africa seems to have been Latin speaking from the first : the great Latin fathers, Tertullian, Cyprian, Augustine, were members of the African Church ; and Africa, not Rome, was the cradle of Latin Christianity.

By the time of Tertullian, from whom we derive nearly all our knowledge on the subject, *i.e.*, at the close of the second century, the Christians were very numerous in every place in North Africa in all ranks of society. The Scriptures, or certain books of them, were early translated there into Latin for the use of these Latin-speaking Christians. In

---

[1] It may be well to point out to some readers the wide difference between Egypt and Pro-consular Africa (now Tunis and Algiers). The civilization of the former was of Greek, of the latter, of Latin origin and character ; the former may be regarded as part of the Eastern, the latter of the Western Empire.

the words of Augustine,[1] "any one in the first
ages of Christianity who gained possession of a Greek
MS., and fancied that he had a fair knowledge of
Greek and Latin, ventured to translate it." The
exigencies of the public service must have necessitated
the early use of a tolerably complete collection of
the books of Scripture, whether a revised selection
from these individual efforts, or an entire and independent translation; and there seems, in fact, to
have been a popular Latin version of the Bible
current in North Africa in the last quarter of the
second century. It was characterized by a certain
rudeness and simplicity, and exact literalness of
translation; and had already been long enough in
circulation to have been able to mould the popular
language.

This recognised version, known by the name of
the Old Latin Version, which could not have dated
long after the middle of the second century, was
jealously guarded for ecclesiastical use, and retained
its position long after Jerome's version was elsewhere
almost universally received. But while the earliest
Latin version was thus long preserved in North Africa
with conservative tenacity, in Italy the familiarity of
the Roman Church with the Greek originals made
them less disposed to cling to the Latin version
as authoritative, while the provincial rudeness of the
version was distasteful to Roman ears. Thus, in the
fourth century, a definite ecclesiastical recension
(of the Gospels at least), by reference to the Greek,

---

[1] De Doctr. Christ. ii. 16.

appears to have been made by authority in North Italy, and was known as the Italic Version. St. Augustine recommends this version[1] on the ground of its close accuracy and its perspicuity, and continued to use it even after Jerome's version had got into circulation.[2]

By the end of the fourth century the text of the Latin Bibles current in the Western Church had become deteriorated by the intermixture by copyists of these various versions; the need of a new version was sensibly felt; and Damasus recognised in Jerome one whose learning and genius qualified him for the task. That the bishop was not mistaken in his estimate of Jerome's abilities, we have the evidence of Professor Westcott,[3] who says that "this great scholar, probably alone for 1500 years, possessed the qualifications necessary for producing an original version of the Scriptures for the use of the Latin churches."

Jerome fully admitted the desirableness of the revision :—" There were," he says in his preface to the work, "almost as many forms of text as copies." Mistakes, he says, had been introduced "by false

[1] De Doctr. Christ.. ii. 15.

[2] There are reasons for believing that other recensions were made in Ireland (Britain), Gaul, and Spain. Professor Westcott (art. Vulgate, 'Smith's Bible Dictionary'), in enumerating the MSS. which establish the fact of a distinct British version, says,—"They stand out as a remarkable monument of the independence, the antiquity, and the influence of British (Irish) Christianity."

[3] 'Smith's Dictionary of the Bible,' art. Vulgate, to which we are indebted for the notices here and subsequently of Jerome's Scriptural works.

transcription, by clumsy corrections, and by careless interpolations," and in the confusion that had ensued the one remedy was to go back to the original source. His avowed aim was to revise the Old Latin, and not to make a new version ; still his corrections of the popular texts were so numerous and considerable, and his version in consequence so manifestly differed from those with which the people were familiar, as to excite against him a wide and deep popular prejudice.

About the same time Jerome also undertook a revision of the Psalter, by comparison with the Greek of the Septuagint. It seems, from his own avowal and from internal evidence, to have been only a cursory correction of manifest imperfections, rather than a thorough revision of the book. It was probably made on the request of Damasus for the liturgical use of the Roman Church, whence it obtained its name of the Roman Psalter, and it continued in use in that Church down to the year A.D. 1566, when Pope Pius V. introduced the general use of the Gallican Psalter, though the Roman Psalter was still retained in three great churches—the Vatican Church at Rome, the Cathedral of Milan, and St. Mark's at Venice.

CHAPTER IX.

THE SPIRITUAL DIRECTOR.

A.D. 382–385.

THE characteristic work of Jerome's three year's residence in Rome was not, however, his share in the conduct of the business of the see, or his critical labours on the Scriptures, but his teaching of asceticism, and his influence upon the society of Rome.

We have already sketched that proud and wealthy and luxurious patriciate; we have seen how, under the initiation of Athanasius, an ascetic school sprang up in the midst of it, whose place of reunion was the palace of Marcella on the Aventine. That patriciate still lived on its brilliant life of frivolity and dissipation, and that school of ascetic ladies still flourished in the midst of it.

We have seen that when Jerome came up to the Council, he was received as the guest of Marcella. That learned and brilliant lady, the first of the great ladies of Rome to adopt the ascetic life, was still the centre and leader of the school. Albina, her mother, who at first opposed her plans, and would have had her accept the distinguished second marriage which Cerealis offered her, had long since followed the example of her daughter's life, and now assisted her religious and charitable labours. Some other new names appear in the circle; among them Marcellina,

G 2

the sister of Ambrose, the great Bishop of Milan; and
Asella, an aged matron, less learned and brilliant than
Marcella, but of a riper judgment, to whom all looked
up as to a mother. A group of distinguished men,
too, were allied with these religious women. Pammachius, the brother of Marcella; Oceanus; Flavius
Marcellinus, an imperial official, who in after years
was delegated by the Emperor Honorius to preside
over the great conference held at Carthage between
the Catholics and Donatists; Domnion, an aged
priest. We name Paula and her daughters last,
because, from their long and close connection with
Jerome, they demand a fuller introduction.

Paula's family was of the highest distinction, claim-
ing descent on the father's side from the Scipios and
Gracchi, on the side of her Greek mother, from the
semi-fabulous kings of Sparta. She had been married, at an early age, to Toxotius, who, like many of
the Roman nobles, still adhered to the worship of the
ancient gods of Rome. Julius Festus Hymetius,
who held considerable offices in the State, and is
commemorated by Ammianus Marcellinus, was her
husband's brother; his wife was the sister of Vettius
Pretextatus, already mentioned as having been appointed prefect of Rome by the Emperor Valentinian,
to restore peace to the city, distracted by the riots
which followed the election of Damasus; and these
three near connections were also pagans. Pretextatus,
we know, was the friend of Symmachus, the chief of the
Senate, the most famous orator of his time, who
headed a deputation of the Senate to Gratian in 382,
and again to the young Valentinian two years after-

wards, to plead against the removal of the altar of
Victory from the Senate-house, the withdrawal of
the State support from the old religion, and their
privileges from its ministers. Thus born, and thus
connected, and the possessor of immense wealth,
Paula was among the greatest ladies of the Roman
aristocracy, and during her husband's life she had
mixed freely in the half-pagan half-Christian circle of
the highest Roman society, living as that luxurious
society lived, only noted as an example of the antique
chastity and dignity of a Roman matron.

Paula had been lately left a widow at the age of
thirty-five, with five children, four daughters, Blesilla,
Paulina, Eustochium, Rufina, and one boy, called
after his father, Toxotius. At first overwhelmed with
grief, she had at length sought consolation in religion ;
had attached herself to the company of her friend and
relative, Marcella ; and when Jerome came to Rome,
he found her among the patrician devotees who
frequented the Aventine palace.

Blesilla, her eldest daughter, after seven months of
an unhappy marriage, had been left a widow, at the
age of twenty, and was rather disposed to banish the
remembrance of her married life in the pleasures of
society than to mourn her husband. Paulina, of a
grave, thoughtful, and affectionate character, was
her mother's stay and comfort. Eustochium, the
third, had been in childhood confided to the care of
Marcella, had been brought up in her palace, and
even shared her chamber ; and, at an early age, had
declared her desire to adopt the life of a church
virgin. She was the first young lady of rank in

Rome to take such a step. Rufina and Toxotius were children who hardly yet enter into the history.

To some of this society Jerome had been known, during his former visit to Rome, when he was mixed up with the affairs of Melania. He was known probably to all by his writings ; his letter to Heliodorus, for example, we know had been circulated among them, and greatly admired by them. When, at the request of Damasus, he resolved to continue in Rome, he also, at the invitation of Marcella, continued to reside in her house; and fell at once into the position of teacher and spiritual director of the patrician devotees who made her house the centre of their society, and of leader of the ascetic party in the Church of Rome. His learning, his own ascetic spirit, and his experience of the ascetic life peculiarly qualified him for the task. Greek was spoken among the upper classes of Roman society as French is with us, some of these learned ladies even knew something of Hebrew, or were glad to learn it under Jerome's instruction. The study of the Scriptures formed a large part of their religious life, and they entered into it with new interest and profit under the guidance of the most learned Biblical scholar of the West. His study of Origen, too, and of other writers of his school, had made him a master of that mystical interpretation of Scripture for which people of the ascetic temperament seem to have a natural predisposition. The influence of this new teacher gave a new impulse to the ascetic spirit in Rome, which soon made itself felt in various directions. A remarkable conversion drew universal attention to the progress of the movement.

The gay and fashionable young widow, Blesilla, was attacked by fever, which brought her to death's door. In the crisis of the disease she had, as she believed, a vision of the Saviour, who touched her, and bade her "rise and go forth," and from that time the fever left her. She believed that her cure was miraculous, and she resolved to devote her life to Him who had thus drawn her out of the jaws of the grave. She at once renounced the world, assumed the habit of a church widow, remodelled her household after the pattern of that of Marcella and Paula, and changed her mode of life. Her high social position, and the dramatic circumstances of her conversion, attracted attention, and made a commotion in society. If the ascetic party was delighted and edified, the world was scandalized, and found fault. Jerome took up his pen in defence of Blesilla, and of the state of life into which she had entered, in the form of a letter to Marcella, which soon found its way into all the palaces of Rome.

This is his account of her vision :—

"God has permitted Blesilla to be tormented for thirty days with a violent fever, in order to teach her not to pamper a body which is soon to become food for worms. . . .

"Jesus came to her and touched her hand, and lo! she arose and ministered to Him. She stank somewhat of negligence, and was buried in the graveclothes of riches, and lay in the sepulchre of this world. But Jesus groaned, and was troubled in

spirit, and cried, saying, ' Blesilla, come forth,' and
she arose and came forth, and eats with Christ. The
Jews threaten and swell, and seek to kill her, the
Apostles alone glorify Him. She knows that she owes
her life to Him who has restored it ; she knows that
it is her duty to embrace His feet at whose judgment-
seat she lately feared to stand. Her body lay almost
inanimate, imminent death shook her breathless
members. Of what use, then, was the help of her
relations ; what was the good of their words, vainer
than smoke ? She owes you nothing, O unkind
kindred ; she is dead to the world, and lives to Christ.
He who is a Christian let him rejoice ; he who is
angry shows that he is not a Christian.

" A widow, who is loosed from the bond of a husband has nothing to do but to persevere. But her
dark-coloured robe offends people ! Let them also
be offended at John, than whom there was not a
greater among men born of women, who is called an
angel,[1] [messenger] and who baptized the Lord,
because He wore a raiment of camel's hair, and a
leathern girdle about his loins. Her poor food displeases them. But it is not poorer than locusts." Then
he breaks out into a retort of savage power. The
widow's pale face and brown robe offend heathen eyes,
he says ; " and they offend Christian eyes who paint
their cheeks with rouge, and their eyelids with anti-
mony; they whose plastered faces, too white for human
faces, look like those of idols, and if in a moment of
forgetfulness they shed a tear, it makes a furrow in

---

[1] Mark i. 2.

flowing down the painted cheek ; they to whom years do not bring the gravity of age ; who dress their heads with other people's hair, and enamel a bygone youth upon the wrinkles of age, and affect a virgin timidity in the midst of a troop of grandchildren.   Our dear widow, in other days, adorned herself with fastidious care, and was consulting her mirror all day long, to see if anything was wanting to set off her beauty.[1] Now she says with confidence these words of the Apostle : ' We all, with open face, beholding, as in a glass, the glory of the Lord, are changed into His image, from glory to glory, by the Spirit of God ' (2 Cor. iii. 18).   Formerly a bevy of handmaidens dressed her hair, and her innocent head was tortured with an elaborate coiffure, now she is content to cover it with a veil.   Formerly, feather beds seemed hard to her, and she could hardly sleep on a couch piled up with them ; now she rises betimes to prayer, and precenting the Alleluia to the rest with ringing voice, she is the first to begin the praises of the Lord.   Her knees press the naked earth, and floods of tears wash her cheeks, once daubed with unguents. . . . Silk robes have given way to a scanty brown tunic, and common

[1] A passage in Plautus's play, the ' Pœnulus,' describes how the whole day of a Roman lady was frittered away in bathing, polishing, painting, and such operations of the toilette.

Ammianus Marcellinus, lib. 28, ch. viii. describes the gentleman going to the bath with thirty attendants, using the finest linen to dry himself, having a whole wardrobe brought, out of which to select the clothes he will use, putting on his rings again, which a servant has been holding lest the hot water should injure them.   Where he lodged, and what bath he frequented, were the ordinary subjects of gossip with a stranger.

sandals replace the gilded shoe, and the finery has been sold to feed the poor; in place of the girdle of plates of gold and precious stones, a woollen cord loosely restrains her robe. If any serpent, with honied voice should try to persuade her to eat again of the forbidden fruit, she would strike him to her feet with an anathema, and say to him, as he writhed in the dust, 'Get thee behind me, Satan,' which, being interpreted, is adversary, for he is the adversary of Christ, and antichrist, who is displeased at the precepts of Christ."[1]

[1] Ep. xix. ad Marcellam.

CHAPTER X.

THE CONTROVERSY WITH HELVIDIUS AND JOVINIAN.

A.D. 382–385.

WE can imagine the commotion which all this must have created in Rome. All the town must have rung with it; and the scathing satire of the Pope's secretary must have made the ears of all the ladies of Rome tingle. Such a defence of the ascetic movement, by a natural consequence, intensified the opposition to it; and the popular feeling found champions in Helvidius, a layman and lawyer, and in Jovinian, who himself had tried the experiment of the ascetic life in a community of monks in Rome. Each published a book on the subject; and each book was answered as it appeared, by the redoubtable champion of asceticism.

Helvidius took the "common-sense" line of argument, if with coarseness, yet not without skill and force. He saw that the perpetual virginity of the Blessed Virgin Mary was the key of the position, and directed an elaborate argument against it. We need not enter into the details of the discussion. It is impossible, from Scripture, to prove either one side or the other. The reasoners against the doctrine of "evangelical perfection" will always be able to assert (but not to prove) that Mary, after the miraculous birth of her firstborn, fulfilled the ordinary life of a holy wife and mother. The instinctive reverence of the Church at large, from the earliest ages to the present day, has assumed (without being able to prove) that a like instinctive reverence in Joseph and Mary preserved the virginity of the mother of our Lord.[1]

We subjoin an extract from Jerome's reply to Helvidius,[2] and we desire to say a word on the motive with which we have chosen this and some other of the extracts in these pages. The two most salient features of Jerome's life-work are (1) that he was the first great teacher of asceticism in the Western Church, and (2) that he was the author of the Vulgate version of the Bible. The latter was beyond all comparison his greatest work; but the influence of his ascetic teaching has been felt continuously throughout the Western world from that day to this; and we have thought it right, in a sketch of his character, and work, and times, to make such selections as would give a fair idea of

[1] The earliest and most general tradition, first recorded by Papias (contemporary with the Apostle John), defended here by Jerome, and accepted by Augustine and the Latin Church generally, is that James, and Joses, and Judas, and Simon, who are called the brethren of our Lord (Matt. xii. 49; xxi. 46, &c.) were strictly his first cousins, being the sons of Alphæus or Clopas and Mary the sister of the Virgin. A second tradition, accepted by Hilary, Epiphanius, and the Greek fathers generally, is that they were the sons of Joseph by a former marriage: Jerome (Com. on Matt. xii. 49) slights this as a mere conjecture, borrowed from the "deliramenta Apochryphorum": Origen says that it was taken from the apocryphal Gospel of St. Peter.

[2] De perpetua virginitate B. Mariæ, adversus Helvidium.

the nature of that teaching, though we guard ourselves against the supposition that we approve all that he says. Moreover, it happens that embedded in ascetic passages are some of the most graphic pictures of the manners of the age.

"§ 20. And since I am about to draw a comparison between virginity and marriage, I beseech my readers not to think that I have disparaged marriage in praising virginity, or made any severance between the saints of the Old and New Testaments, that is, between those who had wives and those who have kept themselves from the embraces of women; for indeed they were under one dispensation suited to their days; but we, under another, upon whom the ends of the world are come. (Verum pro conditione temporum alii eos tunc subjacuisse sententiæ, alii nos, in quos fines seculorum decurrerunt.) Whilst that law remained, 'Increase and multiply and replenish the earth' (Gen. i. 28), and 'Cursed is the barren who does not bear children in Israel' all married and were given in marriage, and leaving father and mother, became one flesh. But when that voice sounded 'The time is short;' it goes on 'let them that have wives be as though they had none' (1 Cor. vii. 29). And wherefore? Because 'He that is unmarried careth for the things that belong to God, how he may please God; but he that is married careth for the things that are of this world, how he may please his wife.' 'And there is difference also between a wife and a virgin; she who is not married careth for the things of God, that she may be holy both in body and in spirit. But she that is married careth for the things of the world, how she may please her husband' (Ibid. 32, 33). What do you clamour at? What do you fight against? The Vessel of Election says these things, declaring 'There is a difference between the woman and the virgin.' See how great her happiness, who has even lost the name of her sex. A virgin is not now called a woman. 'She who is not married careth for the things of the Lord, that she may be holy in body and in spirit.' It is the definition of a virgin to be 'holy in body and in spirit;' for it is no profit to her to have the flesh virgin if she is married in her spirit. 'But she that is married careth for the things of the world, how she may please her husband.' Do you think it is the same thing to spend days and nights in prayer and fasting, and to enamel her face against her husband's return, to trip to meet him, to feign caresses? One, to appear less pleasing, obscures the gifts which nature has given her. The other paints herself before the mirror, and, in contempt of Him who made her, tries to make herself more beautiful than she was born. Thence come infants who cry, and servants who clamour, and children who hang about your neck; you are anxious about expenditure, and guarding against losses. Here a band of aproned cooks bray the meat, there a troop of embroideresses chatter. Presently a servant announces that the master has come in with his friends. The wife flutters like a swallow all about the house to see that the couch is smoothed, the pavements swept, the cups crowned with garlands, the dinner ready. Tell me, I pray, where in all this is there any thought.

of God? And these are happy homes. In others, where the timbrel sounds, the flute squeaks, the lyre tinkles, the cymbal clashes, what fear of God is there? The parasite brags and backbites, takes pride in invective; the victims of lust[1] come in and exhibit themselves to lascivious eyes. The unhappy wife either enjoys all this, and perishes, or she is offended at it, and her husband scolds. Thence arise quarrels, then divorces. But if there is any house free from such things as these—a 'rara avis'—yet the management of the house, the education of the children, the attentions to the husband, the superintendence of the servants, how they call her off from thoughts of God. 'It ceased to be with Sarah after the manner of women,' says the Scripture (Gen. xviii. 11); after which it is said to Abraham: 'In all that Sarah shall say unto thee, hearken unto her voice' (Gen. xxi. 12). She who is as Sarah . . . . ceases to be a woman; she becomes free from the curse of childbirth; her desire is not to her husband, but on the contrary, her husband is subject to her, and the voice of God bids him, in all that Sarah says to thee, hearken unto her. . . .

"§ 21. I do not deny that wives and widows may be found who are holy women; but it is they who cease to be wives; who in married intercourse imitate the chastity of virgins. This is what the Apostle,

---

[1] "Slave women were employed in various ways . . . most frequently they were used at banquets to dance before the festive gentlemen, and to sing, play the lyre, and amuse them with witty sayings."—Dr. Donaldson on the characters of Plautus.

Christ speaking in him, briefly testifies : 'The un-married cares for the things of God, how she may please God ; but the wife cares for the things of the world, how she may please her husband.' Yet he imposes no necessity or bond upon any one, but he persuades to that which is honourable, wishing all to be like himself. And yet, although he had not commandment from the Lord about virginity—because it is beyond men, and it would be too much to com-pel them contrary to nature, and to say I desire you to be as the angels are ; therefore also the virgin has the greater reward, because she despises that which if she had done she would not have sinned—never-theless, he says, I give my judgment, as one that hath obtained mercy of the Lord, to be faithful. I suppose, therefore, that this is good 'for the present distress, that it is good for a man so to be.' What is this distress ? 'Woe unto them that are with child, and to them that give suck in that day' (Matt. xxiv. 19 ; Mark xiii. 17). The forest grows on purpose to be cut down, the field is sown on purpose to be mown. Now the world is full, and the land does not hold us. Presently wars will cut us down, diseases will carry us off, shipwreck will drown us, and yet we are quarrel-ling about boundaries. 'Of this number are those who follow the Lamb' (Rev. xvi. 4), 'who have not defiled their garment, for they have remained virgins.' Note what 'they have not defiled ' means. I should not have dared to explain it if Helvidius had not given a false meaning to it. But you say some virgins are tavern girls : I say more, that some of them are harlots; and what you will still more wonder at, some

clerics are tavern-keepers, and some monks are shame-
less. But who is there who will not at once understand
that no tavern girl can be a virgin, no adulterer can be a
monk, and no tavern-keeper a cleric? Is it the fault
of virginity if a pretender to virginity is a criminal?
Certainly—to leave the other persons and speak of
virgins—if any one is engaged in such occupations,
whether she remains a virgin in body, I know not;
but this I know, she is no longer a virgin in spirit."

Jovinian, the ex-monk, argued against asceticism
on theological grounds. He, like Helvidius, disputed
the perpetual virginity of Mary. He maintained that
virginity, marriage, and widowhood were of equal
merit; and went on to accuse the advocates of celibacy, abstinence, and poverty, of Manicheism; he
argued against the over-estimation in which martyrdom was held.

Some of his arguments will find an echo in the
minds of modern readers, for he argued against the
increasing reverence paid to martyrs and their tombs
and relics; against the keeping of the vigils of
the saints; against the custom of burning tapers
in the daytime, and other similar customs. We obtain, in the course of the controversy, many interesting notes of the ecclesiastical customs of the period.[1]

But he went further than this. "He maintained
that there was no other distinction between men

---

[1] *E.g.* on the antiquity and meaning of the lights on the
altar:—"There are tapers lighted through all the Churches of
the East when the Gospel is to be read, how brightly soever
the sun may shine; not, forsooth, to drive away darkness, but
to declare our joy by that symbol."

than the grand division between the righteous and the wicked, that there was no difference of grades in either class, and that there would be no difference of degree hereafter in rewards and punishments. Whosoever had been truly baptized had nothing further to gain by progress in the Christian life, he had only to preserve that which was already secured to him. But the Baptism which Jovinian regarded as true was different from the sacrament of the Church ; indeed he altogether set aside the idea of the visible Church. The true Baptism he said was a Baptism of the Spirit, conferring indefectible grace, so that he who had it could not be overcome by the devil."[1]

Jovinian's teaching was very acceptable, then as now. The opponents of the ascetic party were elated. Some even, of both sexes, who had embraced the celibate life, abandoned it. Jerome did not content himself with the task of exposing Jovinian's false theology, and defending virginity as one of the states of life to which some were specially called; he attacked Jovinian himself with violent personalities. He asserted the merit of celibacy in such exaggerated language as to alarm his own friends and the friends of his cause, for the consequences of his indiscretion. His friend Pammachius endeavoured to persuade him to suppress his book; Augustine wrote another, 'On the Good of Marriage,' in order to moderate its effects.

[1] Robertson's ' History of the Christian Church.

CHAPTER XI.

THE MIRROR OF THE CLERGY.

A.D. 382–385.

IN the days when paganism was the acknowledged
religion of the state, and the Christian body was
as a whole poor and liable to persecution, and
the clergy were especially liable to be sought out as
victims, these circumstances afforded guarantees that
the clergy would be men of earnest faith and would
lead self-denying lives. But, when Christianity became the religion of the empire, and the piety of
wealthy devotees enriched the clergy, and their office
gave them social consideration, then the character
of the clergy deteriorated; many became proud and
luxurious, and to support their pride and luxury,
in the absence of any sufficient endowments, they
became covetous of gifts and legacies. The Emperor
Valentinian endeavoured to check the scandal by an
edict which prohibited the clergy from receiving
legacies. But Jerome tells us that the edict was evaded,
and the scandal continued. "The priests of idols,"
he says, "players, charioteers of the circus, harlots
even, can freely receive legacies and donations, and it
has been necessary to make a law excluding clerics and
monks from this right. Who has made such a law?
the persecuting emperors? No; but Christian emperors. I do not complain of it. I do not complain
of the law, but I complain bitterly that we should

have deserved it.   Cautery is good ; it is the wound
which requires the cautery which is to be regretted.
The prudent severity of the law ought to be a protection, but our avarice has not been restrained by it.
We laugh at it, and evade it by setting up trustees."[1]

The wealth and luxurious manners of Rome aggra-
vated all these evils there ; and among all classes
of the clergy, priests, deacons, and monks, Church-
widows, and Church-virgins, was an amount of worldliness and luxuriousness which scandalised the whole
Church, and especially excited the reprehension of
the ascetic party within it.   The bishop sympathised
with this party, and was very desirous of restraining
the faults of his clergy.   Jerome's ascetic spirit burned
within him, and when the fire kindled within him he
was never slack to speak with his tongue.

Eustochium, the daughter of Paula, took the veil
of a virgin.   It was a great occasion, for as we have
already said, she was the first young lady of the
Patrician families who had entered upon this mode of
life.   Jerome addressed a letter[2] to her on the occasion, which was not merely a private letter, but a
careful treatise on Church-virginhood ; and he took
the opportunity to put forth a scathing satire on the
faults and vices of the Christian society of Rome.
The Christian society had hardly ceased to laugh at
the satire of the manners of the high pagan society
which he put forth in his defence of Blesilla, when
this satire, equally brilliant and bitter, fell like a

---

[1] Ep. xcv. ad Rusticum.
[2] Ep. xviii. ad Eustochium de custodia virginitatis.

thunderbolt in the midst of themselves; and the pagans had their turn of laughter at the pictures of the courtly priests with a taste for good society, good dinners, and legacies, and the rich widows who loved living in luxurious self-indulgence, and affected to be devotees and leaders of Church opinion. It is one of the most famous of Jerome's letters, and we here give sufficiently copious examples, both of its ascetic and its satirical portions.

"§ 1. Hearken, O daughter, and consider; incline thine ear; forget also thine own people, and thy father's house, and the king shall desire thy beauty. In this forty-fourth Psalm [xlv. in our version], God speaks to the human soul that, after the example of Abraham, leaving its country and its kindred, it should abandon the Chaldeans, which is, being interpreted, the evil spirits, and live in the land of the living, which the Prophet elsewhere longs for, saying, 'I trust to see the good things of the Lord in the land of the living' (Ps. xxvi. 13). But it is not enough for you to leave your country unless you forget your people and your father's house, so that, having despised the flesh, you may be joined to your spouse. 'Look not back,' he says, 'nor stand still in all the region round about, but save thyself in the mountain, lest haply thou be included.' 'Let him that has put his hand to the plough not look back; he that is in the field let him not return home; nor, after having received the robe of Christ, go down from the roof to take any other garment.' (Matt. xxiv.) Great is the mystery, the Father exhorts the daughter not to be mindful of her father.

Ye are of your father the devil, and the lusts of
your father ye are willing to do' (John viii. 44), he
says to the Jews; and elsewhere, 'He who commits
sin is of the devil.' Born first of such a parent we
are black; and after penitence, not having yet ascended
to the height of virtue, we say, 'I am black but
comely, O daughters of Jerusalem' (Cant. i. 4). I
have quitted the home of my childhood, I have
forgotten my father, I am born again in Christ.
What reward shall I have for this? It follows,
'The King shall desire thy beauty.' This, therefore, is that great mystery. For this a man shall
leave his father and mother and shall be joined to
his wife, and they two shall be, not now one flesh,
but one spirit. Your spouse is not haughty and proud,
he has taken an Ethiopian to wife. As soon as you
desire to hear the true Solomon, and to come to him,
he will tell you all his wisdom, and the King will
lead you into his chamber, and, your hue being
changed in a wonderful manner, that saying will
apply to you, 'Who is this that cometh up in shining
garments?' (Cant. iii. 6; viii. 5).

"§ 2. In writing these things, my dear Lady Eustochium (for I ought to give the title of my Lady to the
spouse of my Lord), I wish you to know, from the very
beginning of my essay, that I am not now about to sing
the praise of virginity, whose excellence you have recognised, and which you have embraced; neither am
I about to enumerate the disadvantages of marriage,
by which comes the pain of child-bearing, the crying
of children, the pangs of jealousy, household cares,
and all things which are commonly considered to be

blessings, but which death snatches from us; for married women also have their rank in the Church: marriage is honourable, the bed undefiled; but I would have you understand that you who are fleeing from Sodom must fear the example of Lot's wife. For there is no flattery in this treatise; a flatterer is a fawning enemy: there will be no display of rhetorical phrases, which, in praising virginity, will place you among the angels, and the world under your feet.

"§ 3. I do not wish your vocation to inspire you with pride, but with fear. You go laden with gold, you must take care of robbers. This life is a race to mortals; here we strive, that hereafter we may be crowned. No one walks safely among serpents and scorpions; and my sword, says the Lord, 'is drunk in the heaven' (Is. xxxiv. 5, 6); and do you expect peace on earth, which brings forth thistles and thorns, which the serpent eats; for our warfare is not against flesh and blood, but against principalities and powers of this world, and rulers of these darknesses, against spiritual wickednesses in heavenly places (Eph. vi. 12).

"§ 5. If the Apostle, a Vessel of Election, and separated to the Gospel of Christ, kept under his body, and brought it into subjection, because of the thorns of the flesh, and the solicitation of vices, lest preaching to others, he himself should be found reprobate; if he, nevertheless, saw another law in his members warring against the law of his mind, and himself a captive to the law of sin, if he, after nakedness, fastings, hunger, prison, scourgings, and tortures, coming to himself, cries out, ' O wretched man that

I am, who shall deliver me from the body of this
death?' (Rom. vii. 24), do you think that you ought
to be careless? Take care, I pray, lest one day God
should say of you, 'The virgin of Israel is fallen, and
there is none to raise her up' (Amos v. 2). I say
boldly, though God can do all things, He cannot
raise up a fallen virgin. He is able, indeed, to par-
don her fall, but not to give her the crown of virginity. Let us fear, lest that prophecy be fulfilled in
us 'the good virgins faint' (Amos viii. 13). Observe
what he says, 'good virgins,' because there are bad
virgins. 'Whosoever looketh upon a woman to lust
after her has committed adultery with her already in
his heart' (Matt. v. 28). Virginity then can perish
in the mind. Such are the bad virgins; virgins in
flesh, and not in spirit; foolish virgins who, having
no oil, are shut out by the Bridegroom.

"§ 13. I am ashamed to say how many virgins
daily fall, how many Mother Church loses from her
bosom, stars upon which the proud enemy places his
throne;[1] how many rocks [hard hearts] he hollows out,
and dwells like a dove in their windows . . . .
These are they who are in the habit of saying 'to
the pure all things are pure.' 'My conscience is
sufficient for me,' 'God only desires a pure heart.'
'Why should I abstain from food which God created,
to be used.' And, when they have flooded themselves
with wine, joining sacrilege with drunkenness, they
say, 'Be it far from me that I should abstain from the
blood of Christ.' And when they see any one pale

---

[1] Isaiah xiv. 13.

and sad, they call her a wretch and a Manichean ; and with reason, for fasting is heresy with them. These are they who walk about in public to attract attention, and with stolen glances draw a crowd of young men after them. They deserve to have whispered in their ears the words of the prophet, 'She makes to herself a whore's forehead, she refuses to be ashamed' (Jer. iii. 3). A little purple in their habit, their hair loosely looped up—but so as to allow a tress to escape, a common shoe, a purple scarf floating over their shoulders, short sleeves fitting to the arm, and an affected gait ; this is all their claim to virginity. They have their admirers, so that under the name of virgins they can sell themselves for a higher price. We are very willing to have the dislike of such people.

"§ 14. It is a shame to speak of it; so sad it is, but true ; whence did this plague of agapetæ [1] come into the Church ? whence came this name of wife without marriage ? . . . . It is of such persons that Solomon speaks with scorn in the Proverbs, saying, 'Who shall carry fire in his bosom and his clothes not be burned, or walk upon coals of fire and his feet not be burned?' (Prov. vi. 27, 28).

"§ 15. Having rejected and dismissed these people who desire not to be but to appear virgins, now I

---

[1] It had become common for persons who were vowed to continence, to form spiritual connections with one another of so intimate a kind that they sometimes lived together in the same house. The unmarried clergy especially often had a female inmate. Sometimes the intimacy was carried to a great length. In the letter to Rusticus, Ep. xcv., are some further illustrations of this abuse in the Church of Gaul.

direct all my discourse to you; you, who are the first
of the noble families of Rome to take the vow of
virginity, you must strive the more earnestly not to
lose the good things both of this world and the next.
You have, indeed, learned the troubles of married
life, and the uncertainty of the marriage state, by an
example in your own family, since your sister, Blesilla,
your superior in age, your inferior in vocation, was a
widow in the seventh month of her married life. O
wretched condition of humanity, and ignorant of the
future; she lost both the crown of virginity and the
happiness of married life. And although her widowhood retain the second rank of chastity, yet what
grief do you think she feels continually when she sees
in her sister what she herself has lost, and while she
abstains from pleasure with more difficulty, yet has
less reward of her continence. Yet let her also be
glad, and rejoice, a hundredfold and sixtyfold is the
reward of chastity.

"§ 16. I wish you not to frequent the company of
married women, not to visit patrician houses,[1] not to
be always seeing the things which you have despised
in choosing the life of a virgin. If the wives of judges
and dignitaries are accustomed to expect compliments, if people flock to the wife of the Emperor,

---

[1] He elsewhere sketches the interior of one of these houses:
—"Enter this palace, pass through the crowd of slaves on stair
and in ante-rooms, and at length you are introduced to the rich
widow Sempronia. She is indisposed, and is taking the bath
in the midst of women each more coquettish than the other.
The saloon is redolent of exquisite perfumes. . . . . And
Sempronia calls herself a Christian!"

to pay their respects to her, why should you lower the dignity of your Spouse? Why should you, the spouse of God, be in haste to visit the wife of a man? Learn, in this respect a holy pride, know that you are their superior. It is not only that I wish you to decline the company of those who are puffed up with their husband's dignities, who are hedged in by a crowd of eunuchs, who wear cloth of gold; but avoid also those whom necessity, not choice, has made widows; not that they ought to have desired the death of their husbands, but that when they had the opportunity of living a continent life, they did not embrace it of their own goodwill. They have changed their habit, but not their desires. A troop of eunuchs and servants surrounds their litters, and from their rosy cheeks and plump persons you would rather suppose they were seeking husbands than that they had lost them. Their houses are crowded with flatterers and feasters. The clergy themselves, who ought to maintain the reverence due to their office, and the deference due to their guidance, kiss their foreheads (capita),[1] and stretch forth their hands—you would think to give a benediction, if you did not know that it was to receive a present. They, meantime, who see their priest thus craving their patronage, are puffed up with pride.

"§ 17. Let those be your associates who are given to fastings, whose face is pale, whose age and mode of life make them suitable companions, who daily sing in their hearts, 'Where dost thou feed, where

---

[1] A token of respectful affection.

dost thou lie at noon' (Cant. i. 6); who say from the
heart, 'I desire to depart and be with Christ' (Phil.
i. 23). Be obedient to your parents; after the example of your Spouse; rarely appear in public, visit
the martyrs in your chamber. If you always gad
about whenever there is a reason for it, you will never
be at a loss for an excuse. Be moderate in food.
There are many who are sober in wine, but are
intemperate in food. Read much, learn as much as
you can by heart. Let sleep overtake you in the
midst of your studies, and the sacred Scriptures
pillow your drooping head.

. . . .

§ 19. Some one will say, Do you dare to disparage marriage, which God has blessed? I do not
disparage marriage when I prefer virginity to it. One
does not compare evil with good. Marriage is
honoured when it is placed next after virginity. 'Increase,' He says, 'and multiply, and replenish the
earth.' Let him increase and multiply who is going
to fill the earth; but your flock is in heaven. . . .
Let him marry who eats his bread in the sweat of.
his brow, whose land brings forth thistles and thorns,
and whose grass is choked by briars. My seed shall ·
bring forth a hundredfold.[1] 'All cannot receive the
Word of God but they to whom it is given' (Matt.
xix. 11). Let others be eunuchs of necessity, I, of
my own will. There is a time to embrace, and a
time to abstain from embracing, a time for collecting

[1] The reward of virginity was said to be a hundredfold; of
widowhood, sixtyfold; of married life, thirtyfold.

stones, and a time for scattering them. . . . Let them
sew robes, who have previously lost the unsewn robe;
let them take pleasure in the crying of infants, who, at
their first coming into the world, mourn because they
are born. Eve was a virgin in paradise, marriage did
not come till after the coats of skins. Your country is
paradise. Keep yourself as you were born, and say,
'Turn to thy rest then, O my soul!' (Ps. cxxiv. 7.)
And that you may know virginity to be natural to
man, and marriage to be a result of the fall, marriage
produces virgins, returning in the fruit what it had
lost in the root. 'A rod shall go forth from the root
of Jesse, and a flower shall arise from his root' (Isa.
xi. 1). The mother of our Lord is the rod, simple,
pure, uncontaminated, with no bud upon it, and after
the likeness of God, fruitful of Herself.[1] The flower
of the rod is Christ, who says, 'I am the flower of
the field, and the lily of the valley' (Cant. ii. 1).
And in another place, he foretells 'the stone, cut out
of the mountain without hands' (Dan. ii.), which
signifies that a virgin should be born of a virgin.

. . . .

"§ 20. I praise marriage, because it brings forth
virgins; I gather a rose out of thorns, gold out of
earth, a pearl from a shell. He who ploughs, will
he plough all day? will he not delight himself with
the fruits of his labour? Marriage is the more honoured when that which is born of it is loved
the more. Why do you grudge your daughter O

---

[1] *I. e.*, As God the Father alone begot the Word without any
mother, so Mary alone gave birth to Jesus without any husband.

mother? She was born of your womb, and nourished
with your milk, and brought up in your bosom. You
have kept her a virgin with careful piety; are you
angry because she prefers to be the wife of a king
rather than of a soldier? She offers you a great privilege, to be the mother-in-law of God.[1] 'Concerning
virgins,' says the Apostle, 'I have no commandment
from the Lord' (1 Cor. vii. 25). Why? Because
that he himself was a virgin was not of command, but
of free will. For they are not to be listened to who
pretend that he had had a wife, for when discoursing
of continence, and persuading to perpetual chastity,
he says, 'But I would ye were all as I am' (1 Cor.
vii. 8); and again, 'But I say to the unmarried and
widows, it is good for them if they so remain, even
as I also do;' and in another place, 'Have not we
power to lead about women, as also other Apostles?'
Wherefore, then, has he no commandment from the
Lord about virginity? Because it is of greater merit
that it should not be of compulsion, but of free will.
For, if virginity were commanded, marriage would
seem to be abolished, and it would be very hard to
compel men against nature, and to demand from
men the life of angels, and to condemn, in some
. measure, that which has been ordained.

"§ 22. [He excuses himself from setting out at
length the inconveniences of marriage, because he
has already done it in his book against Helvidius.
He refers the reader to that and to other writings on

---

[1] The passage is not omitted, because without some such
extracts the teaching of Jerome could not be fully represented.

the subject.] Consult the treatise of Tertullian, to a philosopher, of his acquaintance, the two books which he has written on virginity, the fine work of holy Cyprian on the same subject, the books of Pope Damasus, as well in prose as verse, and the treatise which holy Ambrose, a little time ago, drew up for his sister.   There is in this last work so much method, and order, and eloquence that its author has forgotten nothing which could be added in praise of virgins. But I am following another course, since I am not now writing an eulogium of virginity, but teaching you what to do to maintain it.

"§ 27. Take care not to be taken with a desire of vainglory . . . When you give alms, let God only see it ; when you fast, let your countenance be joyful.   Let your dress be neither over neat nor over mean, and not conspicuous by any strange fashion (nulla diversitate notabilis), lest you attract the attention of the passers by, and get pointed at. . . Do not wish to seem more religious and more humble than is needful ; do not seek glory in seeming to avoid it. . . . I do not admonish you not to be proud of your wealth, not to boast the nobility of your birth, not to set yourself before others.   I know your humility, I know that from the heart you say, ' Lord, I am not high-minded, I have no proud looks' (Ps. cxxx. 1).   I know that both in you and in your mother, pride, by which the devil fell, has hardly any place.   Therefore, it is unnecessary to write to you about such things, for it is foolish to teach things when she you teach already knows them.   But do not let this very thing, that you have despised the pride

of the world, generate pride in you; do not,
now you have ceased to pride yourself in golden
robes, begin to take pride in shabby ones; do not,
when you come into a meeting of brethren, or of
sisters, go and seat yourself in the lowest place.　Do
not speak in a faint voice, as if you were half dead with
fasting, and affect a feeble gait, and lean upon some-
body's shoulder.　For there are some who 'disfigure
their faces, and appear unto men to fast;' who, when
they see any one coming begin to groan, cast down
their eyes, and cover their faces, so that they hardly
leave an eye to see with.　Their robe is brown, and
their girdle of leather, and their feet and hands soiled,
only their stomach, which nobody can see into, is
filled with food.　Of such as these the Psalmist says,
'God shall break the bones of them that please men'
(Ps. liii. 6).　There are others who are ashamed to
be women as they were born; they wear men's clothes,
cut their hair short, and walk about shamelessly,
looking like eunuchs.　And still others, who affect
the simplicity and innocence of infancy, dress themselves in elaborate hoods, and make themselves look
like owls.

"§ 28. But lest I should seem to find fault with
women only; avoid those men whom you see wearing
iron chains, with their hair long, like women, contrary
to the command of the Apostle, with a goat's beard,
a black cloak, and bare feet, pinched with cold.
These things are all tokens of the devil.　Rome,
awhile ago, had to complain of such a one in An-
timus, and more recently in Sophronius, men who
gain entrance into the houses of the nobles, and

deceive silly women, laden with sins, always learning,
and never coming to the knowledge of truth, who
affect gravity, and make long fasts, by taking food
secretly by night.   I am ashamed to say more, lest
I should seem rather to rail than to admonish.
There are others (I speak of men of my own
order), who take the priesthood and diaconate
for bad purposes.   All their anxiety is about their
dress, whether they are well perfumed, whether
their shoes of soft leather fit without a wrinkle.
Their hair is curled with the tongs, their fingers
glitter with rings, and they walk a-tip-toe, lest
the wet road should soil the soles of their shoes.
When you see them you would take them for
bridegrooms rather than for clerics; whose whole
thought and life it is to know the names, and houses,
and doings of the rich ladies.   One of these men, who
is the prince of this art, I will briefly and concisely
describe, in order that when you know the master
you may the more readily recognise his disciples.   He
hastes to rise with the sun, he arranges the order of
his visits, he seeks short cuts, and the troublesome
old man almost pushes his way into the bedchambers
of people before they are awake.   If he happen to see
a cushion, a pretty napkin, or piece of furniture, he
praises it, he admires it, he handles it, he complains
that he lacks such things; and he not so much begs
it, as extorts it: for every one fears to offend the city
newsman.   Chastity he hates, fasting he hates; what
he likes is the smell of dinner, and his weakness is—
sucking-pig.   He has a barbarous and forward tongue,
always ready for bad language.   Wherever you go, there

I

he is ; whatever news you hear, he is either the
author or the exaggerator of the report. He is constantly changing his horses, and from their sleekness
and fire you would think that he was the son-in-law of
the Thracian king."[1]

These bitter satires, of course, provoked a great
clamour against the audacious satirist.

In answer to the outcry, he writes a short letter of
two paragraphs, addressed to Marcella. In the first
paragraph he makes the general defence that the
surgeon who probes and cauterizes the wounds of his
patients is not an enemy, but a friend. "Paul, the
Apostle says, 'Am I become your enemy because I
tell you the truth?' and because the Saviour uttered
some hard sayings, many of His disciples departed
from Him. No wonder that when I also attack vices, I
offend many." In the second paragraph he applies
himself to a certain Onasus of Segesta, who had been
foolish enough to take Jerome's satires as pointed at
himself. "I threaten to cut off an offensive nose : the
man with a wen on his is in a fright. I choose to
scold a chattering little crow : and the old crow re-
members that his voice is a little hoarse. Is Onasus
of Segesta, the only man in Rome who swells out his
cheeks with empty words? I say that some have
attained honours by crime, by perjury, by treachery :
what is it to you who know yourself innocent? I
laugh at an advocate who makes stupid speeches :
what is that to you who are learned and eloquent?

Diomed, of whose horses Lucretius says :
' Et Diomedis equi spirantes naribus ignem.'

I choose to rail at priests who have heaped up riches : since you are not rich, why are you enraged? I want to burn Vulcan in his own fires : since you are neither his guest nor neighbour, why should you care to extinguish the flame? I amuse myself by laughing at the grubs, the owls, and the crocodiles, and you take all that I say to yourself. When I attack a vice, you fancy that I am attacking you. . . . Let me give you·a piece of advice. ·Conceal one or two things and you will make a better appearance. Don't let your nose be seen on your face, and don't let your tongue be heard in speech, and then you may seem both handsome and learned!" Portions of this chapter are coarse, but as parts of a picture they are necessary to give a true idea of Jerome's character and of the character of his age.

CHAPTER XII.

THE DEATH OF BLESILLA.

A.D. 382–385.

THUS three years passed on. All this time Jerome retained the habit of a hermit, a brown tunic and robe of like colour, and lived the abstemious life of one, and held no official position except that of secretary of the bishop; but he had become the most conspicuous ecclesiastical person in the Church of Rome, the acknowledged leader of the most influential party in it. He himself believed, and doubtless the belief and hope were shared by many of his friends, that in case of a vacancy no one was more likely to be elected to fill the Roman See.

But the party opposed to him was numerous, and bitter in its enmity. The aristocracy hated the Dalmatian monk, who had become the director of the devotees; the clergy, whose vices he had satirized, were embittered against him; the feeling of the lower classes also was against the ascetic. Just at this time, in Nov. 384, an event happened which fanned the general opposition into a flame. Blesilla's health again gave way, and her sickness had a fatal termination. People were ready enough to say that Jerome and her mother were the causes of her death by the austerities they had made her undertake. Her relations gave her a splendid funeral, a great crowd collected to see the procession pass along the streets, and out of the Capena Gate, and along the Appian Way to the mausoleum of her family. Paula, according to the Roman custom, followed her daughter to the tomb. On the way, her grief overcame her, she broke out into a passion of tears and cries, and at last fainted away, and they were obliged to carry her back to her palace like one dead. This tragic incident produced a great sensation among the spectators. " See this mother," cried one, "who weeps for the daughter whom she has killed with fasting. Let us drive the cursed race of monks out of the city; let us stone them; let us throw them into the Tiber." " It is they who have led this miserable mother astray," said another; "they have compelled her to become a nun, and one proof that she was forced into it is, that she bewails her children as no pagan mother ever did."

Paula did not recover her self-command; she continued overwhelmed with grief; and the sinister reflections upon her conduct continued to injure the cause of religion. Jerome, at length, betook himself to his pen, and addressed a letter to her in which tender consolations were mingled with firm reproofs, and which is a masterpiece of feeling, of taste, and of eloquence.[1]

He begins, " Who shall give to my head water, and to my eyes a fountain of tears, and I will weep—

---

[1] Ep. xxii. ad Paulam.

not like Jeremiah, the wounds of my people, nor,
like Jesus, the miseries of Jerusalem, but I will
bewail sanctity, pity, innocence, chastity, I will
bewail all the virtues which have died with Blesilla."
He goes on to draw a touching picture of her youth,
her talents, her virtues, the pathetic scene of her
death, her gorgeous funeral.

"But what am I about," he says; "I undertake
to dry a mother's tears, and I am weeping myself!
I confess my grief; this whole book is written in
tears. Jesus also wept for Lazarus, because He loved
him. How shall I play the part of consoler when
I am overcome by my own groanings, when my
words are broken by my emotions and choked with
my tears. O, my Paula, I call Jesus to witness, whom
Blesilla now follows, I call the holy angels to witness
whose company she now enjoys, that I suffer the
same grief you do; I, who was her father in the
spirit, and her nurse in charity; I too sometimes
say, 'Let the day perish in which I was born' (Jerem.
xx. 14) . . . .

"Do you think that I too do not feel such thoughts
passing through my mind? Why do wicked old
men enjoy the riches of the world? Why is youth
and sinless childhood cut down like a flower before
it has blossomed? How is it that the child two or
three years old, and the very suckling, is possessed
by a demon, is filled with leprosy, is devoured with
scrofula, while the impious, adulterers, man-slayers,
sacrilegious, blaspheme God, in perfect health and
prosperity . . . . and I have said, 'therefore, have I
cleansed my heart in vain, and washed my hands in

innocency, &c. ?' . . . . God is good, and all things
which the Good does are necessarily good . . . . Let
us rejoice that Blesilla has passed from darkness to
light ; and, while yet in the fervour of her first faith,
has received the crown of a finished work. If, indeed,
premature death had snatched her away while she
was concerned only with the love of the world and the
pleasures of this life, there would be cause to mourn
and bewail her with a fountain of tears ; but when,
by Christ's mercy, she had been baptized hardly
four months, and had thenceforth lived, treading the
world under foot, and always contemplating a
monastic life, are you not afraid lest the Saviour
should say, 'Are you angry, Paula, because your
daughter has been made My daughter ? Do you
despise My judgment, and envy My possession of
her with rebellious tears ? Do you know what I
design for you and for those who remain to you ?
You deny yourself food, not for fasting, but from
sorrow. I do not love such abstinence ; such fasts
are hateful to Me. I receive no soul which quits the
body without My will. Let a foolish philosophy have
such martyrs as these. Let it have Zeno, Cleombrotus,
Cato. My spirit rests only upon the humble and
meek, and them who tremble at My word (Is. lxvi. ;
juxta, LXX.). Is this the monastery you promised Me,
that differently dressed from other matrons, you might
seem to yourself more religious than they ? The
mind which complains belongs to the silk robe. . . . .
If you believe that your daughter lives, you ought
not to complain that she has gone to a better world.
This is what I commanded, by My apostle, that

you should not grieve for those who sleep, as the Gentiles do."

As he draws towards the end he reproaches her for the scandal her unrestrained grief had caused. " I cannot, without deep sorrow, say what I am about to tell you. When they carried you insensible from the midst of the funeral procession, these were the things the people muttered among themselves : ' Is not this what we have often said ; she weeps for her daughter, dead of fasting. How long shall it be before this detestable race of monks is driven out of the city ? Stone them ; throw them into the river. They have led astray this wretched matron ; that she did not wish to be a nun is proved by this, that no pagan ever wept so much over her children,' How much sorrow do you think such words caused Christ? How much exultation to Satan ? . . . I say not these things to terrify you, God is witness, as if I stood before His Judgment-seat, but in these words I exhort you. These tears, which have no moderation, which are bringing you to the threshold of death, are hateful; they are full of sacrilege, most full of faithless-ness. You howl and cry as if they were burning you with torches; you are, as far as in you lies, destroying your own life. But the merciful Christ comes in to you and says, Why weepest thou ? the damsel is not dead but sleepeth (Mark v. 39 ; Luke viii. 52). The bystanders mock Him, that is the unbelief of the Jews. To you also, if you linger about the tomb of your daughter, seeking her, the angel will say, Why seek ye the living with the dead?

" Blesilla cries to you who are weeping for her, ' If

you ever loved me, mother, if you nourished me, if I
was formed by your counsels, do not envy my glory;
do not act so that we shall be for ever separated.
You think me alone : I have, instead of you, Mary,
the mother of the Lord. I see many here whom I
formerly knew not. O, how much better is this
company. I have Anna, who once prophesied in
the Gospel, and, what I more rejoice in, her reward
of the labours of so many years I have obtained in
three months. I have received a palm of chastity.
Do you pity me because I have left the world? But
I mourn their lot whom the prison of the world still
confines; whom, daily fighting, now anger, now avarice,
now lust, now the temptations of many vices allure
to their ruin. If you desire to be my mother, take
care to please Christ. I cannot recognise a mother
who displeases my Lord.' These and many other
things she says, but I cease, and pray to God for
you.

.   .   .   .

"So while my spirit reigns in my members, whilst
I enjoy the intercourse of this life, I promise, I
engage, I bind myself, that my tongue shall sound
her name, my labours shall be dedicated to her, my
mind shall toil for her. There shall be no page which
does not speak of Blesilla; wherever the record of
my discourse shall come she shall accompany my
works; and I will teach virgins, widows, monks,
priests, her name; an eternal memory shall recom-
pense the brief duration of her life. She lives with
Christ in heaven, and she shall live on earth in the
mouths of men. The present age will pass away,

other ages will come which will judge impartially   I will place her name in the midst between those of Paula and Eustochium ; in my books she shall find a deathless fame ; she shall hear me always speaking of her with her mother and her sister."

The last sentence is perhaps a little boastful, but it has been fulfilled : the works of Jerome have given immortality to the names of Paula, Blesilla, and Eustochium.

CHAPTER XIII.

JEROME'S DEFENCE.

A.D. 385.

A MONTH after the death of Blesilla, another death occurred which changed the whole course of Jerome's life; Damasus died in December 384. If Jerome and his friends still had any hope of his succeeding to the vacant chair, their expectations were disappointed; Siricius was elected, and Jerome was left without office and out of favour in the new Papal court. It may have seemed to himself and his friends that his usefulness and his fame were baulked by his failure. The truth is, that he would probably have made an indifferent bishop; he had not the tact or temper requisite in a ruler of men; on the other hand, as bishop, he would never have found leisure for the great work—the Vulgate Bible—the most useful he could possibly have done for the Latin Church, and on which his fame rests firmly while the Church shall endure.

Jerome had made many enemies, and now that his powerful protector was gone, he was made to feel the results of their enmity. It broke out first in the shape of a great scandal.

We have seen already that the celibates of the early Church did not consider themselves debarred from special friendships with persons of the opposite sex, such as between persons in the world would have naturally resulted in their marriage. A friendship of this nature had gradually sprung up between Jerome and the Lady Paula, of whom and of her family we have had so much to say. That friendship was of the purest nature, and we shall see that it lasted till death dissolved it. But the coarseness of thought created by the dissolute manners of the period was sure to be utterly incredulous of the innocence of such "Platonic friendships," and the relations between Jerome and Paula created a scandal. Her relatives assumed the worst views of the case, and annoyed her with reproaches. The talebearers of the city entertained society with details of the supposed intrigue. The populace hooted Jerome when he appeared in the streets. A slave of Paula's, to whom some of those stories were traced, was brought to trial. When put to the torture he retracted his accusations, and did justice to the character of his victims. But this of course did not prevent those who wished to believe their guilt from continuing to believe it.

"There is a great deal of human nature in a man," even though he be a Father of the Church; and Jerome had his full share of human infirmities and inconsistencies. It is difficult to repress a smile when we find him, now that he is disappointed of the See, neglected by its present possessor, harassed by his enemies, beginning to think that it had been a mistake to come to Rome; that his true vocation after all was the desert, and making up his mind to "shake off the dust of Babylon, the scarlet whore of the

Apocalypse," as he is pleased now to style the city to whose see he had aspired, and to return to his solitary cell.

Paula also, for some time past, had had a desire to make the then not uncommon pilgrimage to the Holy Land; and the persecution she had lately suffered could only increase her desire to escape from Rome. She resolved to abandon home and country altogether, to build a monastery in the East, and to spend the remainder of her days within its shelter. Melania had already set her the example, and it is not improbable that Jerome and Paula may have had Melania and Rufinus in mind when they arranged their own plans. For Melania, after leaving Rome, was joined by Rufinus; they sailed to Egypt, and visited the monks and hermits of the desert, scattering her gifts with a profuse hand. Then they made the pilgrimage of the Holy Land, and finally built two monasteries on the Mount of Olives, one for men and one for women, over which they still presided.

Jerome, six months after the death of Damasus, quitted the city never to return to it. A crowd of friends attended him to the port, the Senator Pammachius, the Bishop Domnion, Oceanus, Rogatian, Marcellinus, and others. His brother Paulinian, a Roman priest named Vincent, and several Roman monks, accompanied him to share his fortunes.

Paula and her suite did not start on her pilgrimage for nine months after. But when we find that Jerome awaited her arrival at Antioch, and then continued the rest of the journey in her company, we cannot doubt that it was by mutual arrangement.

On the eve of his departure, while waiting to go on board, Jerome penned his defence against his detractors in the form of a letter to the Lady Asella.[1] We give a few extracts from it.

§ 2. I am, forsooth, an infamous person, crafty and slippery; I am a liar, and deceive with Satanic art. That which they would hardly believe of a convicted person, is it more safe to believe—or rather to pretend to believe—of an innocent person? Some people kiss my hands, and slander me with a viper's tooth, they condole with me with their lips and rejoice in their hearts. God has seen them, and laughed them to scorn, and reserved me, His miserable servant, together with them, for the judgment to come. One finds fault with my walk and my smile, another slanders my countenance, another thinks my simplicity suspicious. I have lived among them nearly three years. A troop of virgins often surrounded me. I explained to them the divine books to the best of my ability. Study brought companionship, and companionship friendship, and friendship confidence. Let them say, if they have ever observed in me anything unbecoming a Christian man. Whose money have I accepted? Have I not refused all presents, great and small? Has anybody's gold tinkled in my hand? Have I spoken an ambiguous word, cast a light glance? They object nothing against me except that I am a man, and that objection was made only when Paula proposed to go to Jerusalem. Be it so. They believed my accuser when he lied, let them also

Ep. xxviii. ad Asellam.

believe him when he retracts. It is the same man
who affirmed and denied; he who before declared me
guilty now declares me innocent. And certainly what
a man says under torture is more to be believed than
what he says amidst applauding smiles. . . .

"§ 3. Before I knew the house of the holy Paula
the whole city had only one voice about me. By
almost the universal opinion I was thought worthy of
the episcopate. Damasus, of blessed memory, was
my mouthpiece. I was called holy, I was called
humble, I was called eloquent. Have I ever been
seen to enter under the roof of a woman of doubtful
reputation? Is it silk robes, brilliant jewellery, a
painted face, is it love of gold, which have ensnared
me? Were none of the matrons of Rome able to
move my mind except one who mourns and fasts;
who is squalid with neglect, almost blind with weeping; whom often the dawn surprises after a whole
night spent in praying God for mercy; whose song is
the Psalter, whose speech is the Gospel, whose delights are self-denials, and whose life a fast? Yes, she
only could please me, whom I have never seen to eat,
and from the moment that, for her purity, I began to
venerate her, to seek her acquaintance, to esteem her,
from that moment all my virtues have vanished.

"O envy! whose teeth gnaw thyself first of all!
O subtlety of Satan, always attacking holy things! no
Roman women have been the subject of more gossip
to the city than Paula and Melania, who, trampling
under foot their wealth, and giving up their children,
have raised the cross of Christ as a kind of standard
of piety. If they had frequented the baths, covered

themselves with perfumes, and made their wealth and
widowhood an occasion of luxury and licence, then
they would have been called great and holy ladies.
But they have chosen to make themselves beautiful
in sackcloth and ashes, and to descend into the fires
of Gehenna with fasting and mortifications. Why,
indeed, could not they be content to perish with the
crowd, amidst the applause of the people? If they
had been pagans or Jews who condemned the life
they led, they would have had the consolation of not
pleasing those whom Christ does not please; but,
O shame! they are Christians, who, neglecting the
beam in their own eye, seek for a mote in their
brother's eye. They attack a resolution to lead a
holy life, and imagine it a safeguard against their own
condemnation if no one is holy, if the whole multitude are sinners.

"§ 5. You delight to bathe daily; another thinks
these cleannesses are filthinesses. You fill yourself
to repletion with wildfowl (attagen), and boast of a
debauch of sturgeon; I make a meal of pulse. A
crowd of laughing guests pleases you; the mourning
of Paula and Melania pleases me. You are covetous
of other people's wealth; they despise their own.
You delight in wine flavoured with honey; cold water
is pleasanter to them. You think lost whatever you
cannot possess and eat and swallow down now; they
desire future things, and believe those things true
which are written. Wisely or unwisely, they act on
faith in the resurrection; what does it matter to you?
Your vices, on the other hand, displease us. You
may be fat if you like; I prefer to be thin and pale.

You think such people as we are miserable ; we think you much more so. We return like for like, and each seems to the other to be mad.

"§ 6. I have written these lines, dear lady Asella, on the eve of going on board, in haste, weeping and mourning; and I thank my God that I am worthy of the hatred of the world. Pray that I may return from Babylon to Jerusalem ; that Nebuchadnezzar may not be my lord, but Joshua the son of Josedec ; that Ezra may come (which being interpreted 'r 'helper'), and restore me to my country. Fool that I was, who thought to sing the Lord's song in a strange land ; who deserted the mount Sinai to seek help from Egypt. I did not remember the warnings of the Gospel—that the man who goes down from Jerusalem falls among thieves, who spoil him of his raiment, and he is robbed, wounded, slain; but though the priest and the Levite despise him, the Samari-tan is merciful (Luke x.), who, when they said, ' Thou art a Samaritan, and hast a devil ' (John viii. 48), denied that He had a devil, but did not deny that He was a Samaritan, since what we call a guardian, the Hebrews call Samaritan. They call me a malefactor ; I, a servant of Christ, accept the title. They call me magician ; so the Jews called my Lord :[1] a seducer ; so they called the Apostle.[2] No temptation has taken me but such as is common to man (1 Cor. x. 13). And what is it after all which I, a soldier of the cross, have suffered ? The infamy of a false accusation has been cast upon me ; but I know that it is through

---

[1] Luke xi. 15. [2] Acts xxiv. 5.

good report and through evil report one must come
to the kingdom of heaven.

"§ 7. Salute Paula and Eustochium, mine in
Christ, whether the world will or no ; salute Albina,
my mother, Marcella my sister, Marcellina, the holy
Felicitas, and say to them, we shall all stand before
the judgment-seat of Christ ; there it shall be seen
in what spirit each has lived.   Remember me, illustrious example of purity and virginity, and let thy
prayers smooth for me the stormy sea." [1]

[1] Ep. xxviii. ad Asellam.

CHAPTER XIV.

THE PILGRIMAGE TO THE HOLY LAND.

A.D. 385.

THE history of Paula and her family is henceforward a part of the history of Jerome, and we follow it with interest. Before the winter set in, Paula had completed her preparations for quitting Rome for ever. Eustochium was to accompany her, and a little company of maidens, taken from all classes, destined to form the nucleus of the convent which Paula proposed to found in Palestine. She distributed part of her fortune among her children whom she left behind, and made every arrangement for their welfare. Her children, her brother, her relations, her friends accompanied her to the port. Jerome describes the touching scene of the embarkation, when children and friends strove to shake her resolution with tears, caresses, entreaties, remonstrances, while Paula, silent and tearless, kept her eyes fixed on heaven, as if seeking there for strength. But when on board and the sails began to swell with the breeze, and the ship to leave the quay, and she saw the group of weeping friends, with her young son, Toxotius, stretching out his hands to his mother, and Rufina, silent and motionless, but with imploring eyes fixed upon her, then her strength gave way, and she hid her eyes from the moving spectacle, whilst Eustochium supported and comforted her.

K 2

At Cyprus they made a stay of ten days. Epiphanius, the archbishop of the island, who had been the guest of Paula during the Roman Council, now repaid the hospitality he had received. This distinguished bishop, who will yet again appear in the history, is one of the prominent Churchmen of the period. He was of Jewish parentage, born at Eleutheropolis, in Palestine, and when young had lived in Egypt. These circumstances of birth and residence had, no doubt, contributed to the knowledge of languages for which he was famous—Hebrew, Syriac, Egyptian, Greek, and Latin ; he had an extensive reading, and was, as we have had occasion to notice, famous for his knowledge of the history and tenets of the various heresies which had arisen in the Church. He had in middle age adopted an ascetic mode of life, and built a monastery at Eleutheropolis. Afterwards he had taken up his residence in Cyprus, in a monastery which he built. When a vacancy occurred in the chief see of the island, the people forced the office upon him. He had founded other monasteries in the island, and was held in high estimation throughout the Church for sanctity and learning.

After visiting these monasteries and resting from their fatigues, the pilgrims continued their voyage to Seleucia, and thence ascended the Orontes to Antioch; where they found Jerome and his companions awaiting them, and Paulinus—the bishop declared by the Eastern Council to be a schismatical intruder, and by the Roman Council to be the legitimate Patriarch of Antioch—ready to entertain them as his guests.

Ordinary travellers would, perhaps, have wintered

in the attractive capital of the East ; but Paula was impatient to attain the goal of her desires. The two parties, therefore, of Paula and of Jerome, made up a caravan, the ladies riding on asses, like ordinary pilgrims, with their luggage on pack-mules ; in this humble fashion the daughter of the Scipios continued her progress through Syria, travelling, probably, by the coast route, which is the most practicable in winter. They remained a short time at Cæsarea, which was still the seat of the Count of Palestine and of his provincial government, and continued their journey to Jerusalem.

Judea was already in the fourth century a country of ruins and of desolation, ruins caused by the Jewish wars against Syria and Egypt, ruins caused by the Roman wars against the Jews, lands wasted by the military operations of Titus, and still more, by the revengeful destructions of Hadrian.   No land had been so ploughed with the sword and watered with blood.   Nature itself in this arid climate wore an aspect of sadness, which Jerome notices, and which seemed to the pilgrims in harmony with their notion of it as a land cursed for the sins of its people.

Jerome, with the Bible and Eusebius's description of the holy places in his hands, was the guide of the pilgrims. His own description of their journey forms the second in the long series of accounts of the Holy Land, which stretches from the time of Helena to our own. We do not propose to follow the journey in detail, but only to make an extract here and there which may seem of special interest.

The city which Hadrian had built upon the ruins

of Jewish Jerusalem was a Roman city, which he adorned with two temples, to Jupiter and Venus, and called after his own name, Ælia Capitolina. Constantine had replaced the temples with two grand basilicas on the sites of the Calvary and the Sepulchre. The fashion of pilgrimages, which Helena had set, had attracted a motley population from all parts of the Christian world, and the city had grown in population and wealth. It was possible, from the distance, for the approaching pilgrim to realize in its site and general aspect the city of Herod—the city of Christ; but arrived within its walls, it was a luxurious Roman city, more disorderly and more luxurious than other cities. It was only within the precincts of its grand basilicas that the pilgrim found himself amid sacred associations, as he kissed the Cross of Christ, or knelt at the place where it had stood with its sacred burden, or adored within the sepulchre from which the Lord rose. The governor of the city, learning the approach of so distinguished a person as the lady Paula, sent a guard to meet her at the gate, and escort her to his palace, where he proposed to lodge her; but Paula preferred to retain the humble style in which she had commenced her pilgrimage, rode through the streets on her ass, and took up her residence at her hired lodging. But though they declined the civilities of the prefect of the city, they had other friends in the city, whose affectionate welcome added to the joy of their visit. Melania, and Rufinus, the friend of Jerome's youth, had, as we have seen, been long in their monasteries on the Mount of Olives. Jerome and Rufinus had kept up a correspondence through all the years of their separation, and the reunion of the four friends in Jerusalem was a source of the highest gratification to them all.

Jerome describes the emotion with which Paula beheld and adored the holy places—her enthusiasm was not chilled by the doubts of their authenticity which force themselves upon the modern pilgrim : " She made the round of the holy places (at Jerusalem) with such ardour and earnestness that she could scarcely be induced to leave one except to hasten to the next. Prostrate before the cross, she adored as if she saw her Lord hanging upon it.   In the sepulchre of the resurrection she kissed the stone which the angel removed from the door of the tomb.   What tears, and groans, and mourning she poured out there all Jerusalem is witness, the Lord Himself is witness, to whom she prayed."

From Jerusalem they went to Bethlehem. We shall have to describe the place more fully on the occasion of their second visit to it ; but we wish to extract here Jerome's description of the vivid way in which Paula realized the sacred scenes, and the emotion which they caused her.[1] " I swear to you," she said to Jerome, kneeling beside her, "that with the eye of faith I see the Divine Infant, wrapped in His swaddling clothes. I hear my Lord crying in His cradle.   I see the Magi adoring the star shining from above ; the Virgin Mother ; the careful nursing father ; the shepherds coming by night to see the Word which was made Flesh ; the slaughtered chil-

---

[1] Ep. lxxxvi. ad Eustochium.

dren ; raging Herod ; Joseph and Mary fleeing into Egypt." And with mingled tears and joy, she said : " Hail Bethlehem, House of Bread, where was born the true Bread, which came down from Heaven. Hail, Ephrata—the fertile—whose fruit is God." All the prophetic passages of Scripture came into her memory, she quoted them in Latin, in Greek, in Hebrew, as they occurred to her, and her pious companions taxed their memories with her. "And have I, a miserable sinner," she cried at last, "been accounted worthy to kiss the cradle where my Saviour uttered His first cry ? Have I been accounted worthy to offer my prayers in this cave where the Virgin Mother brought forth my Lord ? Here be my rest, for it is the country of my Lord ! Here will I dwell, since my Saviour chose it," and turning to Eustochium, she added, " and my seed shall serve Him."

The pilgrims took the usual round of Hebron and Mamre, and the Dead Sea, the Mount of Olives and Bethany, Jericho and the Jordan, Sichem and Samaria, Nazareth and the Sea of Galilee, through which we will not follow them ; and returning to Jerusalem prepared for the overland journey to Egypt.

CHAPTER XV.

EGYPT.

A.D. 385.

IT was the political genius of Alexander which discerned, in the little Egyptian town of Rhacôtes, the fitting site for a great city, which should be the capital of his Western conquests. The Ptolemies completed the unfinished city, as the capital of that portion of his Empire to which they had succeeded.

We speak of the city as it existed at the period of our history; three hundred years after the wars of Pompey had added it to the Roman Empire, nearly three hundred years after St. Peter had founded a Christian Church there, and left St. Mark the Evangelist as its bishop. The city was built on a flat strip of land at the Canopic mouth of the Nile, bounded on the north by the sea, and on the south by the Mareotic Lake. The island of Pharos, of white, dazzling calcareous rock, on the north formed a barrier against the waves of the great sea; a long spit of low land on the east formed a natural breakwater on that side; a mole from the middle of the island to the mainland was all that was needed to complete a great harbour at the mouth of the Nile, the only great harbour round all the eastern coasts of the Mediterranean. The famous lighthouse was a lofty tower, 400 feet high, built on a rock, at the very entrance to this harbour. The Mareotic Lake, connected by several canals with the

Nile, formed a great basin for all the interior naviga-
tion of the country, and another canal connected this
basin with the outer harbour.

The city was peopled by a large colony of Mace-
donians, by a large colony of Jews, to whom Alexander offered the same privileges as to his own
countrymen, and by a third large body of native
Egyptians who, however, were not admitted to the
privileges of the Macedonian and Jewish colonists ;
the Roman conquest added a fourth body of Roman
civil officials, a garrison, and merchants.

The city was planned and built with all the large-
ness of conception and magnificence of art which presided over the design of the Greek cities of the East.
One great street, four miles long, ran through the
whole length of the city, from west to east; another, a
mile long, crossed it at right angles, not in the middle, but further westward, at such a point that it gave
upon the great mole which joined the mainland to
the island of Pharos.   These two great streets, 200
feet wide, were adorned with a covered colonnade on
each side, allowing ample space for carriages in the
central roadway.   There was a great square at their
intersection ; and the great gates of the city were at
their terminations ; the Canopic gate on the east, the
Gate of the Necropolis on the west, the Gate of the Sun
on the south, the Gate of the Moon on the north.   The
city was defended in its whole circuit by walls and
towers.   Beyond the city, on the east, was the great
hippodrome, built by Cleopatra.   Beyond the city, on
the west, was the Necropolis, with extensive catacombs,
approached through gardens and vineyards.   The

palace of the Ptolemies, and the smaller palaces of the royal princes, with their groves and gardens, occupied the spit of land which formed the east side of the harbour ; and the small harbour containing the royal galleys and the royal dockyard was in that angle of the great harbour. The Regio Judæorum, the Jews' quarter, occupied the N. E. part of the city ; it was enclosed from the rest of the city by its own walls, and its inhabitants observed their national laws and were ruled by their own magistrates. The Rhacôtis, the native quarter, occupied the S.W. part of the city, and was similarly defended by its own walls. The city had the usual magnificence of public buildings. The Mausoleum called the Soma (the Body), in which rested the remains of the great founder, carried thither on a golden car, escorted by an army, across the lands from Babylon to Alexandria. The Museum, in the Bruchium, the Greek quarter, was a magnificent group of edifices, with its library, botanic garden and menagerie, and formed the university of Egypt. The Romans had added the Cæsarium, where the genius of Cæsar was worshipped. The native quarter had its Serapium, the temple of Serapis, which rivalled the magnificence of the temple of Jupiter, of the Capitol.[1] It was erected on the summit of an artificial mount, raised one hundred steps above the level of the adjacent parts of the city, and the interior cavity was strongly supported by arches, and distributed into vaults and subterranean apartments. The consecrated buildings were surrounded by a quadrangular portico of four hundred magnificent Corinthian

[1] Gibbon

columns, of which Pompey's pillar is the one remaining fragment;[1] and the treasures of the learning of the ancient world were preserved here in the famous Alexandrian Library. The idol itself was a colossal figure of wood, covered over with plates of gold. The city had, besides, its temples, theatres, and public halls, and colonnades of the finest marbles of the Egyptian quarries, and was adorned with obelisks and sphynxes, taken from the old Pharaonic cities of Egypt. The southern and western sides of the harbour were lined with broad quays of granite, with such a depth of water that ships could moor alongside and lade and unlade their cargoes; hard by were vast granaries, in which were stored the harvests on which Rome and Constantinople depended for their food, and a spacious square, surrounded by colonnades, which formed the Emporium, the exchange of Alexandria.[2] It was, moreover, the capital of the learning of the world. It had become

---

[1] If the Arab tradition is to be received.

[2] The hero of the Greek novel of 'The Loves of Clitophon and Leucippe,' by Achilles Tatius (A.D. 500), describes his landing from the Mareotic Canal, entering into the city by the Gate of the Sun, and walking through the street with its two ranges of columns, right and left, till he reached the central square, from which opened other streets of immense length. What he found most admirable was the extent of the city and the multitude of its inhabitants, and the crowds in the public places. "The city appeared so vast in extent that one could not believe it to be filled with inhabitants, and the people were so numerous that one doubted if any city could contain them." Ammianus Marcellinus speaks of its temples standing proudly above the houses, with high lanterns and towers, among which the Serapium overtops the rest. (Lib. 22, ch. xvi.)

to Greek learning what ancient Athens was. Jewish learning had assumed a new vitality in this the greatest and wealthiest colony of that ancient race. And the Catechetical school of Alexandria, under Clement, Origen, and Athanasius, had been, for some centuries, the great school of Christian theological study.

Our travellers were persons of high culture, and quite capable of appreciating all the varied interest of the city, but it was its Christian aspect which specially attracted them. It was to them, not so much the city of Alexander and the Ptolemies, of Anthony and Pompey, as the city of Peter and Mark, of Clement and Origen and Athanasius. The young bishop, Theophilus, who had lately (A.D. 385) succeeded Timothy, gave a courteous reception to the illustrious Roman lady and the distinguished scholar. They found Isidore, who had accompanied Athanasius to Rome years before, now established in Alexandria as master of the Guest-house, and therefore their official host. But Didymus, the master of the famous Catechetical school, seems to have attracted their interest more than any other person. Though blind from his youth, he was famous for the extent and depth of his erudition. Jerome visited him almost daily in order to profit by his learning, and all his life after spoke of the great master with respect and gratitude. Paula, Jerome tells us, always accompanied him to profit by their conversation, and showed even more impatience than himself for these interviews. They lingered here a month before they proceeded to organize their expedition to visit the monks of the Desert, which was the great object of their journey to Egypt.

CHAPTER XVI.

THE FATHERS OF THE DESERT.

IF the reader will look at the map of Egypt, a line drawn from Alexandria to Memphis will pass beside three parallel ranges of mountains running in a S.E. and N.W. direction. These mountain chains enclose two great valleys; the one towards the east is the Valley of the Natron Lakes; the western-most valley is the desert of Sceté; both seem as if at one time they had formed the beds of other branches of the Nile. The Valley of the Natron Lakes is so called because of a chain of lagoons which seem to mark the ancient course of the river; the other valley still bears the name of the Dry River. These two valleys and the mountains which bound them were the scene of that wonderful development of the Christian life which Paula and Jerome and their companions had come so far to see.

They took the route between the sea and the Lake Mareotis, crossed the desert, and so entered the Nitrian Valley by its north-west opening. A thick salt fog filled the valley during the night, and seemed to solidify under the rising sun and fall in little crystals as of hail; sharp crystals of nitre pierced the shoes of the travellers and the sandals of the guides. They threaded their way among marshes, some deep

enough to swallow up man and beast, others breathing forth pestilential vapours when the thick mud was
disturbed. The Nitrian mountain, standing detached
from the Libyan chain, dominated all the valley. Its
summit was crowned by a great church ; on its flanks
were fifty great monasteries ; at its feet was the
ancient town of Natron, with an indigenous population. To this aggregation of habitations had been
given the name of the City of the Lord, or the City
of the Saints. Each of the fifty monasteries was
under the direction of its own superior, but they were
all under the same rule, all under the government of
one abbot, and under the episcopal oversight of the
Bishop of Heliopolis. Either in the town or in the
dependencies of the monastic establishments, were to
be found butchers and bakers, confectioners, wine-
merchants, physicians, and in short all that was
necessary for the convenience of visitors or of sick
members of the monastic community. A dozen miles
south of the valley, in the ravines of the mountains, existed a population of 600 solitaries. They
inhabited natural caves, bowers of branches, subterranean cells, so arranged that they could neither hear
nor see one another, and they held no communication
with one another. These cells were dependencies of
the City of the Saints, and had no other church than
that upon the summit of the Nitrian mountain.

At a distance of a day and night's journey across
the dividing range of hills was the Valley of Sceté.
Its monastery was probably situated on a terrace of
the hills. Nitria was an Eden compared with the
utter desolation of this arid valley, enclosed by barren

hills. Not a drop of water, not a blade of verdure was to be seen; the blinding glare of the Egyptian sun poured down upon it all day long, and all the year round. It needed a fierce ardour of devotion to enter upon its life, a firm resolution to persevere in it.

The Bishop of Heliopolis had been informed of the visit of Paula and her company. He had himself gone to the mountain with a number of his clergy to welcome them, and had prepared a great reception for them. As the travellers began to ascend the mountain the bishop began to descend in order to meet them, surrounded by his clergy, by a multitude of monks, and by a company of the hermits. All ranged in order, the procession descended the mountain singing psalms and hymns. The bishop saluted Paula, who modestly replied, "That she rejoiced in his welcome to the glory of God, but felt herself unworthy of such honour." The bishop placed his distinguished visitors beside him, and the procession wound up the mountain-side to the great church at its summit.

The church was large enough to contain the whole number of cœnobites and solitaries, who all attended divine worship here every Saturday and Sunday; if one was absent, some of the brethren went directly after service to see what had happened to him, for nothing but death or some great sickness prevented their attendance. Eight priests, assisted by deacons and subdeacons, were attached to the service of the church, but the chief of them alone said mass, gave the exhortations, and decided upon all spiritual questions. If any one had received a letter which he thought interesting to the brethren, he showed it to this priest first, who decided whether it should or should not be read to the assembly. Jerome admired this perfect order, so much beyond that of the monasteries of Syria. Near the church they noticed three palm-trees, every one with a stick hung from one of its branches. The visitors were told, in reply to their questions, that, according to the rule of Macarius, the founder of the community, these trees served for whipping-posts for those who merited such punishment. The first was reserved for monks convicted of any breach of rule, the second for robbers if any should be found in the country, the third for fugitives from justice.

While walking around the plateau of the mountain they saw seven mills employed in grinding corn for the convents. They saw also a house where there seemed to be a great confusion. They were told that it was the Guest-house, where the community entertained visitors. The rule was, that strangers might live there as long as they liked, weeks or months or even two or three years; but at the end of the first week they had tasks assigned them for the service of the monasteries; one was sent to the bakery, another to the garden, another to the kitchen. To educated people a book was given to read, and they were requested not to speak before noon.

The interior rule of the monasteries, which they could not witness, was explained to them. "These men, so strictly imprisoned," they said, "place their happiness in their sequestration, so that when the affairs of the community make it necessary to send one of the brethren on an errand, each tries to excuse himself, and he who accepts the commission does it as an act of obedience."

Bidding adieu to the City of Saints, our travellers journeyed on to the suburb of the Cells, the abode of the anchorites.

The reader will have observed how the narrative has led us through all the stages of the ascetic life, beginning with the elegant asceticism of the *salon* of Marcella, whose noble ladies led a-life of abstinence and study and contemplation in gilded saloons, surrounded by troops of servants, retaining possession of princely wealth; then to the mild celibacy of the monasteries of Epiphanius, in the delicious scenery and climate of Cyprus; so rising to the ruder life and greater privations of the monks of Chalcis and of the neighbouring solitaries; but there, it will be remembered, the monks ran gossiping from monastery to monastery; and Jerome himself had scribes in his cell with whom he prosecuted his studies, and received visits from neighbouring solitaries, with whom he carried on theological and literary conversations. In the City of the Saints we have perhaps the most fully organized type of the monastic constitution; but it is in its dependent cells that we arrive at the highest ideal of the ascetic life. It is here that we find the men who have gone to the very limits of human endurance, in the endeavour to get away from the world, to subject the flesh, and to place the soul habitually alone face to face with God. Here human enthusiasm revels without restraint, and exhibits the wildest eccentricities of fanaticism. Every cell has its own character, and every hermit indulges his own ideas of devotion.   One has built his hut among the rocks of a projecting peak, another has excavated his cavern in the bowels of the earth ; one exposes himself without shelter under the blazing sun, another has excluded himself altogether from the light of day; one has walled himself up in his cell and never leaves it, another wanders about without any settled abode. Their costumes are as various and as wild as their habitations.   One is wrapped round with the skin of a beast, and with his shaggy uncombed hair and blackened meagre countenance, looks himself like a wild beast ; another wears from neck to heel a tight garment of platted water-flags ; one a rough shapeless sack of haircloth, another nothing but a cloth about his loins.

Jerome and Paula visited among the cells, seeking out especially those famous hermits, the heroes of this spiritual warfare, whose names were spoken with reverence throughout the world.   Antony, and Paul, and Pachomius, indeed were dead, but Serapion, Arsenius, Macarius, were still alive.

Serapion inhabited a cavern situated at the bottom of a chasm, to which they descended by a steep stair amid a thicket of bushes.   The cavern was hardly large enough to contain a bed of dry leaves ; a plank wedged in a crack of the rock formed his table ; an old Bible laid upon this table, and a cross, clumsily carved, hanging against the rock, formed all the furniture of the dwelling.   The tenant of this den looked more like a browned skeleton than a living man   His hair covered his face and shoulders, his body looked like that of some tawny beast; his only clothing was a piece of cloth wound about his body. This strange person had known Rome in former days, spoke Latin well, and took pleasure in conversing about the patrician families with whom he had been acquainted. His history was not less extraordinary than his present appearance. During his youth, while he lived in the Eternal City, he had conceived a great pity for two comedians, a man and woman, who were living in all the licence of their profession, and resolved to restore them to a better life by means of the true faith. With this view he sold himself to them as a slave, and plunged in their train into this disorderly life, from which he desired to withdraw them, as one casts one's self into the sea in order to save a drowning person. The holy enterprise was crowned with success. Thanks to his remonstrances, his counsels, his prayers, his masters abandoned their dishonourable mode of life; they became Christians, and were baptized. They desired to enfranchise the slave who had converted them, but Serapion would not accept this favour. He presented himself before them with some pieces of money in his hand. "My brethren," he said to them, "before quitting you in search of such other adventures as God may call me to, I bring you this money.; it is the price you gave for me; it belongs to you: as for me I carry away the gain of your souls." After long consideration he resolved to remove to Egypt and bury himself in the awful solitude of the desert.

They heard the stories of some of the old hermits who had passed away to their reward. Pambon, who had been visited by Melania a few years before ; it was related, that when she entered his cell she caused her servants to lay at his feet a quantity of silver vessels as a gift. Pambon, without even looking at them, bade the disciple who waited on him " Carry these to our brethren of Libyia and of the Isles, who are poorer than we are." Melania said, " Do you know, my father, that these vessels contain three hundred pounds weight of silver?" He cast a glance of rebuke upon her, and replied, " God, who weighs the mountains and forests in His balance, needs not that you should tell Him the weight of your silver ; and as for me, I have nothing to do with such things. Do not forget, my daughter, that God reckoned the two mites of the widow a greater offering than all the gifts of the rich." They showed the travellers the cell where this and that great hermit lived, the tree planted by one, the tool used by another : they told them of their sayings, their visions, their miracles, which the one told and the other heard with equal good faith and entire credence.

" With wonderful enthusiasm," says Jerome, " and a courage hardly credible in a woman, forgetting their sex and their weakness, she had a desire to settle with her young nuns among all these monks (for female convents, and even female solitaries, were not unknown in the desert), and perhaps she would have done it had not the love of the holy places had a still greater attraction for her." Accordingly, they returned to the port of Pelusium, there took ship for Maiüma, the port of Gaza, and thence returned to Bethlehem.

CHAPTER XVII.

BETHLEHEM.

A.D. 386–389.

BETHLEHEM, the scene of the beautiful pastoral of Ruth, the birthplace of David, the place of the nativity of our Lord and Saviour, is situated on a long, grey limestone hill, which lies east and west, and is about a mile in length. The hill has a deep valley on its north and south sides ; on the west, the ridge sinks gradually down into the valley, but towards the east it terminates in a bold rocky bluff, which overlooks a plain of several miles in extent. The slopes of the hill are formed artificially into terraces, which sweep round the contour of the hill with great regularity, and are planted with vines, and olives, and figs. The village stands on the top of the hill ; and outside it, to the eastward, on the edge of the steep descent, stands the ancient Church of the Nativity, built by Helena ; and the vast pile of Byzantine building, more like a fortress than a monastery, which still represents the convents of Paula and Jerome.

The Cave of the Nativity is, perhaps, the most authentic of all the series of holy places ; and the church which still stands over it is the most perfect example of the churches which the Empress Helena and Constantine the Great built on the traditional sites of the great events of the Gospel history.

The Khan of Bethlehem was a well-known place in the time of the Gospel history, for it was the place

CHURCH OF THE NATIVITY.

where the travellers rendezvoused to form themselves into caravans, for mutual protection on the journey down into Egypt. The spot within it, or in its precincts, in which the Lord was born, could not but have been held sacred by Christians, and kept in memory among them. The Emperor Hadrian seems to have tried to discredit Christianity by erecting temples and statues on the sites regarded by the Christians as specially sacred. Thus, on the site of the Calvary and the Holy Sepulchre, at Jerusalem, as we have said before, he erected two temples, one to the Jupiter of the Capitol, and the other to Venus.   And here at Bethlehem, he planted a grove and erected a shrine and statue of Adonis at the place of the Nativity.

Justin Martyr, about the middle of the second century, is our earliest authority for the existence of a tradition that our Lord's birth took place in a certain cave very close to the village (Justin. 'Dial. cum Tryphone,' 78).   And, in the next generation, this seems to have been the constant tradition of the place, even among those who were not Christians (Origen c. Cels. i. 51).   So that the spot was reverenced by Christians as the birthplace of Christ two centuries before the conversion of the empire, and before that outburst of local religion which is commonly ascribed to the visit of Helena.[1]   When the Empress Helena sought for the traditional sites of the Gospel history, this cave was pointed out to her as the place of the Nativity; and Eusebius (who wrote within seventy years of the time) tells us that she found here Hadrian's statue of Adonis.   She ordered the erection of a church over the site; Constantine seems to have added to the sumptuousness of the church, but Mr. Fergusson considers the nave of the existing church to be part of the original work of Helena, and an almost unaltered example of a church of that age.   This nave is 215 feet long, by 103 feet across, divided into a body and double

[1] Stanley.

aisles by four rows of monolith columns, with
capitals of Corinthian character, and a flat ceiling
of beams of cedar from Lebanon. The present choir,
with its three apses, does not seem to be part of the
original arrangement, but to have been added by
Justinian when he renovated—Eutychius (erroneously)
says rebuilt—the church.

From the choir of the church the pilgrim descends
by stairs into the crypt, which is an excavation in
the rock. Immediately beneath the choir is an
irregularly-shaped chapel, dimly lighted with silver
lamps, the offerings of various ages and nations, containing two small recesses nearly opposite one another.
In the floor of the northern recess is a slab of marble,
inlaid with a silver star, with an inscription round it,
HIC·DE·VIRGINE·MARIA·JESVS·CHRISTVS
NATVS·EST. The southern recess, which is a few
steps deeper than the floor of the chapel, is the manger
in which the new-born Babe, wrapped in his swaddling
clothes, was laid. It contains an alabaster trough,
or hollowed bed, made to represent the manger and
to replace it.[1] This is enclosed within a shrine, hung
with blue silk, and embroidered with silver. Opposite
the shrine of the manger, and but a few yards
from it, is another chapel, where it is said the
three Magi opened their gifts and worshipped. This
is the grotto where the kneeling Paula so vividly

---

[1] According to the mediæval Roman tradition, the actual
wooden manger was discovered here, which is now deposited in
the Basilica of Sta. Maria Maggiore at Rome, and there dis-
played to the adoration of the faithful every Christmas Day.

realized the events of the Nativity on the occasion of her first visit, and conceived the idea of building her monastery, and spending her life here.

The two companies—Jerome, his brother, and his friends; Paula and Eustochium, and the Roman virgins—secured lodgings in the town, and proceeded to mature their plans, and put them into execution. They purchased ground adjoining the Church for the sites of their buildings, viz., a monastery of monks, under the rule of Jerome, two monasteries of women, under the guidance of Paula, and a hospital or guest-house for the entertainment both of pilgrims and travellers, after the example of that which they had seen at Nitria ; so that, Paula said, if Joseph and Mary should again visit Bethlehem they would have a place to lodge in. Paula had wealth enough for the contemplated work, but Jerome resolved to contribute the remains of his patrimony, and sent his brother Paulinian to Aquileia to dispose of it. Then there were the plans of the buildings to arrange, builders to be engaged, materials to be collected, so that three years passed away before the monasteries were ready for their occupants.

Meantime, Jerome obtained possession of a cave near that of the Nativity, and adopted it as his cell, arranged his books and papers, engaged scribes, and commenced the life of diligent study and prolific authorship which only death interrupted. He was now forty-one years of age. Since he had left his parental home at Strido to attend the schools of Rome, he had never been settled for more than three years in one place and in one occupation. Rome, Treves, Aquileia, Antioch, the desert of Chalcis, Antioch again, Constantinople, Rome again, and eastern travel, had filled up the previous one-and-twenty years. The cave at Bethlehem witnessed the next thirty-four years of his life, witnessed his death, and formed his sepulchre. This latter half of his life was not less full of diligent study, of fiery controversies, and was more productive of valuable results, than the former half of his life had been.

He at once laid himself down a rule of religious life, to which he adhered to the end. He retained the simple brown tunic of a hermit, which he had worn even in Rome. He fasted until sunset, and then ate only vegetables and bread ; he allowed himself flesh and wine only in case of sickness. He observed the usual hours of prayer, and the greater part of his waking hours was spent in literary occupations.

In order to confer a benefit on the town where he had taken up his abode, he opened a school, gratis, for the children of the inhabitants. In teaching them Latin and Greek he recurred to the authors, whose books, after his vision, he had forsworn ; and recurred to them with all the delight with which one reads again the favourite books of youth. He applied to Rufinus at Jerusalem to get some of these pagan authors transcribed for him by his monks, and sent to him at Bethlehem. For his own more serious studies he undertook to perfect himself in Hebrew and Chaldee, and so to qualify himself for the important task of making a new version of the books of the Old Testament from the originals. He had been struck with the justice of the objection which the Jews were in the habit of making against the Christians, who pretended to comment upon their sacred books when they did not even know the language. He had been more especially incited to undertake a new translation from the Hebrew into Latin by the suggestion of an Eastern monk, named Sophronius. This monk, in disputing one day with a Jew, quoted a verse of a Psalm out of the Septuagint; but the Jew interrupted him with the assertion that it was a false quotation, that the Hebrew had quite another meaning. There was no denying that in many places the Septuagint seemed to be rather a paraphrase than an exact translation of the Hebrew original; and it was manifest that in argument with Jews, at least, a new version was needed, and that even for the satisfaction of the faithful such a version would be of great value. Sophronius placed this thought before Jerome, as one who was qualified for the important task, offering on his own part that if Jerome would translate the Hebrew into Latin, he would translate Jerome's Latin into Greek for the use of Oriental Christians. There was no lack of learned masters. About the middle of the second century schools of Jewish learning were established in Tiberias, and continued to flourish there during several centuries. The *Mishna* was compiled there in the early part of the third century; the *Gemara* in the middle of the fourth century. Jerome could find, therefore, at Tiberias, if not in Jerusalem, rabbis who had inherited the learning of the older teachers, and who had spent a lifetime in the very studies in which he needed their assistance. It was the custom of these rabbis that each gave himself specially to the study of some particular book of the Scriptures, or some particular dialect. Jerome took pains and incurred considerable cost in obtaining the best assistance ; he mentions particularly a rabbi of Lydda, who united in an eminent degree the love of learning and the love of gold ; another rabbi of Tiberias ; and still another, with whom he studied the Chaldaic dialect of Daniel. The name of one of these rabbis, Barraban, afterwards gave point to one of Rufinus's attacks upon his quondam friend, when, accusing him of turning Jew, he says that after the example of his friends he prefers Barabbas to Jesus.

Jerome had a strong creative impulse within him ; as bees in summer time turn all they gather into honey, so whatever he learned he reproduced in some new literary work. Thus these Hebrew studies bore fruit at once in the production of two books ; one on Hebrew places and names,[1] a topographical work in illustration of the places mentioned in the Bible ; the other an explanation of the meaning of the proper names mentioned in the Bible.[2] He also, at this time, wrote commentaries on several of the Epistles of St. Paul, at the request of Paula and Eustochium ; he also took up again a commentary on the book of Ecclesiastes, which he had begun at the request of Blesilla, had laid aside at her death, and

---

[1] 'Liber de situ et nominibus locorum Hebraicorum.
[2] 'Liber de nominibus Hebraicis.

now completed in affectionate memory of her, and dedicated to her mother and sister. He also, at the request of these two friends, translated the Homilies of Origen on St. Luke, he also translated the treatise of Didymus of Alexandria on the Holy Spirit, dedicating these works, in the interesting prefaces, which he prefixed to most of his works, to his brother Paulinian and his two "sisters" of Bethlehem.

This is the place to speak of the remarkable share which Paula and Eustochium had in the literary labours of Jerome. When we say that they suggested many of the works which he accomplished, it must be understood that he undertook them in the first instance for their own personal instruction, and then for the benefit of his friends and the world. They not only suggested the works, but had a real share in their accomplishment. After making every allowance for the probable partiality of Jerome's estimate of the learning and genius of these two ladies, we must believe that they really possessed so much of learning and of taste that their cooperation in his work had a real influence upon the results. Very soon after Jerome had settled himself with his books and his scribes in the cave, which he called his "paradise of studies," the two ladies had begged to be allowed to come there at certain hours, and that he would read through the Bible with them. Jerome says that Paula had learnt easily and thoroughly that Hebrew language which had cost himself so much labour, and not only had an admirable knowledge of it, but spoke it with a perfect accent.

Eustochium also, he says, attained very soon to the
same perfection.   They both knew Greek as the
language of their maternal ancestors, the language
of the Greek Toxotius, the husband of one, and
father of the other ; in fine, as the language which
formed part of the accomplishments of the Roman
aristocracy.   Paula, says Jerome, knew the Scriptures
by heart, and while she loved their historical sense,
and declared it to be the basis of their truth, she
sought with greater delight the spiritual sense, as
more adapted to feed the spiritual life of the soul.
Her inquiring mind would not be satisfied without
going to the bottom of everything.   "When I in-
genuously confessed my ignorance on any point, she
would not pass over it, but desired to know the
opinions of writers upon it, and my judgment upon
their expositions."   It was amidst these readings,
questions, suggestions, and discussions that the
exact translation of a passage was at length fixed,
or the commentary upon the text was elaborated ;
and that which Jerome at length dictated to his
scribes must often have owed much to the suggestive
questions and elegant taste, if not to the scholarship,
of his collaborateurs.   Jerome delighted to associate
their names with his own in his literary works ; the prophetic truth of the boast, the affectionate desire for
the fame of others as well as his own, redeem the
arrogance with which he declares, apostrophising
Paula, then deceased, " I have wrought a monument
more durable than brass, such as no age can destroy,
that wherever my works shall be read the reader may
know thy praises, thou who art buried in Bethle-

hem."[1]   We have not yet concluded the list of the
works of these three prolific years of Jerome's residence in Bethlehem.   It was probably during this
period that, again at the urgent request of Paula and
Eustochium, he undertook another and more thorough
revision of the Psalter, in which, still taking the Septuagint version as the basis of his translation, he
tried to represent as accurately as possible the real
meaning of the Hebrew.   In this work his fellow-
students undertook, under his direction, the collation
of MSS., and the construction of a corrected text of
the Septuagint version.   This new version soon
obtained a wide popularity.   Gregory of Tours is
said to have introduced it from Rome into the public
services of the churches of France, and from its use
there it obtained the name of the Gallican Psalter.   It
was retained in public use in France from that day
to this, and in A.D. 1566 Pope Pius V. (as has already
been stated) substituted this "Gallican" for Jerome's
earlier "Roman" version in the churches of Italy.
He appears to have proceeded to a similar revision of
the Latin version of the other books of the Old
Testament, restoring them all by the help of the
Greek to a general conformity with the Hebrew; but
the history of this portion of his work is obscure; and
the results of it seem to have disappeared.

The enemies of Jerome pursued him in his retreat,
criticising everything which he did.   When he read
the Greek and Latin classics with his scholars, they
denounced him as an apostate, a pagan, a teacher

Ep. lxxxvi. Epist. Paulæ.

of polytheism, a corrupter of youth. When he was studying Hebrew with his Jewish teacher, they accused him of turning Jew himself. His successive amendments of the text of Scripture excited widespread disapproval, his dedication of his works to women was the subject of sneers. Jerome felt all these attacks keenly, and replied to them with the vehemence and personality and power of satire which are characteristic of his controversial writings.

Defending himself against the charge of mixing together quotations from Cicero and the Bible, he replies, " These people who attack me know as little of the Bible as they do of Cicero, or they would have called to mind that in Moses and the prophets there are many things taken out of the books of the Gentiles. Who does not know that Solomon proposed questions to the philosophers of Tyre, and answered theirs? Has not the Apostle Paul himself quoted, in his Epistle to Titus, a verse of Epimenides against liars? Has he not, in his first Epistle to the Corinthians, inserted a verse of Menander? and in his disputation at Athens, on Mars Hill, cited the testimony of Aratus in the end of a hexameter verse? And what shall I say of the doctors of the Church? They were all brought up on the ancient writers, whom they refuted . . '. These great men had learnt from David to snatch the sword from the enemy's hands, and to cut off the proud Goliath's head with his own blade. They had read in Deuteronomy[1] this precept of the Lord : ' Thou shalt shave the head of the

---

[1] Deut. xxi. 12.

M

female captive, and her eyebrows, and pare her nails, and then thou shalt take her for thy wife.' . . . And what else is it that I have done, having loved the ancient wisdom, and delighted in the charms of her speech, and the beauty of her features, I have taken her as my captive and handmaid, and made her an Israelite."

In answer to those who blamed him for dedicating his works to women, "As if these women were not more capable of forming a judgment upon them than most men," he says in his dedication of the Commentary of Sophronius, "the good folk who would have me prefer them to you in my estimation, O Paula and Eustochium, know as little of their Bible as they do of Greek and Roman history. They do not know that Huldah prophesied when men were silent, that Deborah overcame the enemies of Israel when Barak trembled, that Judith and Esther saved the people of God. So much for the Hebrews. As for the Greeks, who does not know that Plato listened to the discourse of Aspasia? that Sappho held the lyre beside Alceus and Pindar? that Themista was one of the philosophers of Greece? And, among ourselves, Cornelia, the mother of the Gracchi—the daughter of Cato and wife of Brutus, before whom the virtue of the father, and the austerity of the husband paled, do we not count them among the glories of Rome? It would take up whole books to relate all the instances of greatness among women."

CHAPTER XVIII.

LIFE IN THE CONVENTS OF BETHLEHEM.

A.D. 389.

AT length the buildings, so long in progress, were ready for their tenants : great, massive, severe ; half fortress and half monastery ; with a single external door, so low, that those who entered had to stoop almost double ; with external windows only at an inaccessible height ; with a tower at one end of the building, which formed a citadel in which the communities might take refuge from any attack of the wandering Arab tribes.

The little company of Roman virgins, who had all this time been practising the religious life under Paula's guidance, formed the nucleus of the convents of women, and were speedily joined by a crowd of maidens and widows, some rich, some poor, who desired to place themselves under Paula's rule.

Jerome, in his sketch of the Life of Paula, describes their daily life : [1]—

" § 19. I will now speak of the order of her monastery. . . . Besides a monastery of men, which she assigned to be governed by men, she gathered many virgins together out of divers provinces, some who were noble, some of middle rank,

---

[1] Ep. lxxxvi. ad Eustochium.

M 2

and some of the meanest condition; and these she
divided into three bands and three monasteries; but
so that, while separated in their work and in their
food, yet in their Psalms and Prayers they were
joined. As soon as the Alleluia was sung, which was
the sign by which they were summoned to the
assembly, it was lawful for none to forbear coming.
Paula being either the first, or at least one of the
first, would watch the arrival of the rest; provoking
them to be diligent by her example, and by shame
rather than by fear.   In the morning early, at the
third hour, at the sixth, at the ninth, at vesper, and at
midnight, they sang the Psalter in order.   It was not
lawful for any one of the sisters to be ignorant of the
Psalms, or to omit to learn somewhat daily of the
Holy Scriptures.   Upon the Sundays only they went
forth to church, at the side whereof they dwelt, and
every troop followed their own mother; and from
thence returning together, they attended to the work
which was appointed, and made clothes either for
themselves or others.   Those who were noble were
not permitted to have any companion of their own
family, lest, being kept in mind of former things, they
should recall the old errors of their idle youth, and
renew them by often talking of them.   They wore all
the same habit.   They used no linen except for the
wiping of their hands. . .   If any of them came
later to the choir, or were more slack in working than
the rest, she would deal with her several ways.   If
she were choleric, by fair language; if she were
patient, by reprehension; imitating that of the
Apostle : 'What will ye, that I come to you with the

rod or in the spirit of meekness' (1 Cor. iv. 21).
Excepting food and clothes, she permitted none of
them to have anything, according to St. Paul, ' having
food and raiment, therewith be content,' lest by the
custom of having more she should minister occasion
to avarice, which is satisfied with no wealth; the
more it lusts, the more it requires, and is lessened
neither by plenty nor poverty.   Such as have fallen
out among themselves she would reconcile by gentle
persuasions.   She would tame the wantonness of the
younger girls with frequent and double fasts, choosing
rather to let their stomachs suffer than their souls.
If she saw one of them too particular about her
appearance, she would reprove the offender with a
contracted brow and sad face, saying that the affected
cleanliness of the person and clothing is uncleanness
of the soul.   An indecent or immodest word was
never to proceed out of a virgin's mouth, for by those
signs a lustful mind is shown, and by the outward
man the vices of the inward man are betrayed.   If
she observed any one to be a tattler and gossip, or
forward and quarrelsome, and that, being often ad-
monished, she did not amend, she would make her
pray in the hindermost rank, or out of the choir, or
eat alone at the doors of the refectory; to the
end that whom chiding could not mend, shame
might.   She detested theft like sacrilege, and things
which were accounted small faults, or none at all
among secular people, she esteemed great sins in
monasteries.   What shall I say about her piety and
diligence, about sick persons whom she cherished
with wonderful attention and care?   But she, who

liberally afforded all things to sick persons, and would also give them flesh to eat; whensoever she herself was sick, allowed herself no such indulgences; and in that seemed unjust that, being so full of pity to others, she exercised so much severity upon herself.

"§ 20. There was none of the young girls, healthful and strong, who gave herself to so' much abstinence as Paula did, with that broken, aged, and weak body of hers. I confess that in this point she was somewhat too self-willed, for she would not spare herself nor hearken to my admonition."

The monks, who gradually filled the monastery under Jerome's care, were many of them men of learning, and in addition to the usual practices of the ascetic life, study was their principal occupation. Every Sunday they walked in procession to the neighbouring church, where alone the Holy Communion was celebrated, the church being under no control on the part of the heads of the monastic establishments, but depending on the Bishop of Jerusalem, and served by his clergy. The hospital was an important part of the foundations; the continual stream of pilgrims and travellers kept it full; and Jerome complains that the distraction of its care interfered with his studies.

The recluses of Bethlehem kept up a constant correspondence with their relations and friends in Rome. During these three years Paula's second daughter, Paulina, had been married to Pammachius; Toxotius, her son, had grown up like so many others of the Roman aristocracy, a pagan, and a bitter one, full of ridicule and sarcasm against Christians, but he was about to be married to Læta, the daughter of Albinus, the Pontiff, who was herself a Christian, and who soon effected the conversion of her husband.

Marcella's mother, Albina, had recently died. Paula and Eustochium jointly addressed a letter to their friend, urging her to quit Rome and take a share in their life and work in Bethlehem,[1] from which we give some extracts.

"§ 9. It would take too long now to run through each age from the Ascension of the Lord to the present day, and recount who of the Bishops, who of the Martyrs, who of the Doctors of the Church, have visited Jerusalem, esteeming themselves less perfect in religion, and less perfect in science, if they had not received the finishing touch, as they say, of virtues, if they had not adored Christ, in those places where first the Gospel shone forth from the Cross. Indeed, if the distinguished orator [2] thinks him inferior who has learnt Greek at Lilybæum instead of at Athens, and Latin in Sicily instead of at Rome, because each province has something peculiar to itself which others cannot have, why should we suppose any one can have arrived at the height of Christian excellence, except at our Athens?

"We do not say this because we deny that 'the kingdom of God is within us,' and that there are holy men in other quarters, but we especially assert this

---

[1] Ep. Paulæ et Eustochii ad Marcellam, xliv.

[2] Cicero said contemptuously of Quintus Cæcilius, who wished to undertake the cause of the Sicilians against Verres :— "If you had learnt Greek at Athens instead of Lilybæum, and Latin at Rome instead of Sicily," &c.

that they who are foremost in all the world are gathered together here. To which places we have come, not as first, but as last, that we might see in them the foremost from all nations. Certainly the flower and most precious stone among the ornaments of the Church is the choir of monks and virgins. Whoever was first in Gaul hastened hither. The Briton, severed from our world—' *Divisus ab orbe nostro Britannus,*'—who has made any progress in religion, leaving his western land, seeks the place known to him only by report and by the relations of the Scriptures. Why need I mention the Armenians and Persians, the people of India and Æthiopia, and Egypt—prolific of monks, Pontus and Cappadocia, Cœle-Syria, and Mesopotamia, and all the multitudes of the East, who, according to the saying of the Saviour, ' Where the carcase is, thither will the eagles be gathered together,' run together to these places, and display to us the example of various virtues. Their tongues, indeed, differ, but their religion is one. There are almost as many choirs of choristers as there are different nations. Among these (which is the first of virtues among Christians) there is no arrogance, no pharisaical disdain, the only strife is, which can be most humble. The newest comer is the first in estimation. There is no distinction of habit, and no care about it. Wherever any one pleases to go, nobody blames, and nobody praises. Fasts do not exalt any one; neither abstinence is blamed, nor is moderate abundance condemned. To his own master every one standeth or falleth. No one judges another lest he should be judged of the

Lord. And that which is common in some provinces, that they of the same calling quarrel with one another, we are almost entirely free from. Far from luxury, far from pleasure, there are so many places of prayer in the city, that the day is not long enough to visit them all.

" § 10. But to come to the little city of Christ and the lodging of Mary (for every one bestows most praise on what is his own). In what words, with what tone, can we place before you the cave of the Saviour? And the manger in which the Infant cried is more honoured by silence than by futile speech. Where are the broad porticos, where are the gilded ceilings, where the houses furnished by the sufferings of wretched slaves and the labour of convicts, where the palace-like halls erected by private wealth that the worthless little body of a man may walk about more sumptuously, desiring rather to see his own things in good order than the heavens; as if anything in the world could be more ornamental than they? See in this little hole of earth the Maker of the heavens was born, here he was wrapped in swaddling-clothes, here visited by the shepherds, here pointed out by the star, here adored by the magi. And this place seems to me more sacred than the Tarpeian rock so often struck by lightning in token of God's displeasure."

" § 11. Read the Apocalypse of John, and consider what he says of the scarlet woman, on whose forehead are written blasphemies, seated on seven hills amidst many waters, and about the going out from Babylon : 'Go out of her, my people, says the Lord, and be not partakers of her delights, and ye

shall not be partakers of her plagues' (Rev. xviii. 4).
And going back to Jeremiah, listen to a like Scripture: 'Flee out of the midst of Babylon, and save
every one his own soul; for she is fallen, Babylon the
great is fallen, and become a habitation of demons, a
hold of every evil spirit' (Jer. li. 8). There are indeed there the churches and the trophies of the
apostles and martyrs; and true confession of Christ;
there the apostolic faith is preached, though trampled
on by heathenism; and the Christian name is daily
raising itself on high; but there also is ambition,
power, the vastness of the city, to see and be seen, to
compliment and slander, to hear and talk, and to see
a crowd of people; these things are alien from the profession of monks and from peace. For either we see
people who visit us, and we break our silence, or we
refuse to see them, and we are considered proud,
Again, in order to return people's visits we go to
splendid porches, and, amidst the remarks of insolent
servants, we enter gilded doors. But in the little city
of Christ, as we said before, all is rustic. The silence
is only broken by psalms; wherever you turn, the
ploughman holding the plough sings alleluias; the
toiling reaper cheers his labour with psalms; the
vinedresser, pruning the vine with his curved knife,
sings something of David. These are the ballads of
this country, these the love songs, this the shepherd's
pipe, these its rustic sports."

Jerome added a short letter to theirs. After speaking of all the littleness and falseness and misery of a
worldly life, he contrasts with it the life of Bethlehem,
where their bark, long tossed by the waves, and buf-

feted by storms, and threatened with shipwreck by
the rocks, had at length reached a safe harbour :—
" Here bread, and herbs grown with our own hands,
and milk, rural delicacies, afford us humble but
healthy food.   Living thus, sleep does not overtake
us in prayer, satiety does not interfere with study.
In summer the trees afford us shade.   In autumn
the air is cool, and the fallen leaves give us a quiet
resting-place.   In spring the field is clothed with
flowers, and we sing our psalms the sweeter among
the singing of the birds.   When the winter cold and
snow come, we have no lack of wood, and I watch
or sleep warm enough.   Let Rome keep its crowds,
let its arena be cruel, its circus go wild, its theatre
indulge in luxury, and not to forget our friends, let
the senate of ladies exchange their daily visits.   Our
happiness is to cleave to the Lord, and to put our hope
in the Lord God (Ps. lxxii.), that when we shall exchange our poverty for the kingdom of heaven, we may
exclaim, ' What have I in heaven, and what do I desire
on earth, but Thee ?'   When we seek such things in
heaven, we grieve that we ever sought for poor and
perishing things on earth.   Farewell."

CHAPTER XIX.

HIS LITERARY WORKS.

THE whole period of Jerome's life in Bethlehem was full of literary activity. His sight was affected, and he was obliged to spare his eyes, but this hardly diminished the voluminousness of his productions; Paula and Eustochium collated MSS. for him, scribes wrote at his dictation. He was fond of dedicating his labours to his various friends, and the dedicatory epistles are full of personal interest. He was rapid in composition, and was fond of telling · how this was dictated during a sleepless night, and that was the result of so many sittings, and the other was written while the messenger waited for it. It is not necessary here to do more than to give a few notes on the more important or interesting of his works.

His commentaries on the books of the Old and New Testaments must be reckoned among his most important works. The plan of such a book as this which we are writing hardly admits of long extracts of Scriptural commentaries, we therefore desire the more to impress upon the reader that Jerome is recognised, both by ancient and modern scholars, as among the greatest of Biblical scholars and critics, and that his Scriptural versions and commentaries

are the most important of his works, and almost continuously occupied the whole of the years of his
manhood. He brings to bear upon them the whole
treasure of his learning, both secular and religious;
he treats of both the literal and the mystical meaning;
and they are a monument of his learning and ability
and piety.

His controversial works against Helvidius, Jovinian, Vigilantius, Rufinus, and Pelagius are famous
for their dialectical skill, still more famous for their
vigorous invective and unscrupulous personality.
We are not concerned to deny that Jerome sometimes descends to coarseness in his wit, and to
brutality in his personalities, and that we have here
the most unfavourable side of his character.

His treatises on the ascetic life we have already
had occasion to quote from largely. We will only
note here that they cover all the varieties of the religious life. His letter to Rusticus is on the duties of a
monk; to Eustochium on the duties of a virgin; to
Nepotian on the duties of a priest: on the duties of
a widow there are three treatises; the first in a letter
to Furia, the second in a letter to Sabrina, the third
in a letter to Ageruchia. They have exercised a large
influence on the mind of the Western Church from
his own day to the present hour.

His letters are by no means the least valuable of
his writings. Letter-writing, as a form of literary expression, has, for the time, so utterly gone into disuse
among us, that it is almost necessary to remind the
rising generation of readers, that it is a form of
composition which has great advantages for certain

subjects, and which has therefore been adopted by famous writers, from Cicero and Pliny to Horace Walpole and Madame de Stael. These letters of Jerome's are sometimes elaborate essays, sometimes prefaces to his theological works, at other times they are fiery effusions thrown off in a heat of strong feeling; but, always intended for publication and preservation, the letters are to be reckoned among his "Works," and are by no means the least valuable of them. Extending from his early manhood almost to the end of his life, they supply us not only with an autobiography, but also with a vivid picture of the eventful period during which he lived. He received letters from Germany, Gaul, Spain, Italy, Africa, Asia, from friends and strangers, from rich and poor, men and women, on all kinds of religious questions; and he put all the treasures of his learning, his religious experience, and his good sense at the service of his correspondents.

His funeral orations ought not to be passed over without a word of special notice; they are a little elaborate and artificial, perhaps, according to the taste of the time, but they are undeniably eloquent, and have probably afforded models for some of the most striking productions of the same kind in modern times. They are varied in their subjects. Thus there is the letter to Paula on the death of her daughter Blesilla, to Heliodorus on the death of his nephew Nepotian; these two are the most famous. There are also the letters to Theodora on the death of her husband Lucinus, to Pammachius on the death of his wife Paulina; and the funeral elogies on the virgin Asella, the widows Paula, **Fabiola**, and Marcella.

But incomparably the most important of all his works, and that on which his fame securely rests, is his translation of the Old and New Testaments from the original languages.

The history of this new version is told in the main in the prefaces to the several instalments which were successively published.[1] The books of Samuel and Kings were issued first, about A.D. 391 or 392 ; and to these he prefixed the famous *Prologus Galeatus*, addressed to Paula and Eustochium, in which he gives an account of the Hebrew Canon. It is impossible to ascertain why he determined to select these two books for his experiment, for it does not appear that he was requested by any one to do so. The work itself was executed with the greatest care. Jerome speaks of the translation in the preface as the result of constant revision : " Read, therefore, first my Samuel and Malachi ; mine, I say : mine ! for what by frequently revising and anxiously amending we have learnt and hold fast, is ours."

In 393, the sixteen prophets were in circulation,. and the book of Job had lately been put into the hands of his most intimate friends. The next books which he put into circulation, probably in 394, yet with the provision that they should be confined to friends, were Ezra and Nehemiah, which he translated at the request of Dominica and Rogatianus, who had urged him to the task for three years. The

---

[1] Smith's ' Bible Dictionary,' art. Vulgate.

three books of Solomon followed in 398, which were the work of three days, when he had just recovered from a severe illness which he suffered in that year. The Pentateuch followed, probably, after 400; Joshua, Judges, Ruth, and Esther, were completed, at the request of Eustochium, shortly after the death of Paula, which happened in 404 A.D.

If he began about 389, as it appears from the context, he was then but forty-three years old, and if the translation was finished in 404 A.D., he was then but fifty-eight years old.

To appreciate the value and importance of Jerome's great work, we must well weigh these considerations. While Greek was the common language of the East, and was even adopted by the educated classes of Rome itself, Latin was adopted by all the conquered nations of the West, and became the common literary language of all Europe for fourteen centuries. In Pro-Consular Africa, as well as in Italy, Gaul, Spain, and Britain, everybody who could read at all read Latin. It is one of the vulgarest of vulgar errors that the Scriptures were kept in Latin in the Middle Ages to keep them from the people; on the contrary, they were circulated in Latin in order that everybody who could read might read them.

Hebrew was a language unknown even to the learned. The Septuagint version of the Old Testament, since it was used and quoted by our Lord and His apostles, was universally regarded as authoritative, and as having a kind of inspiration. The Latin versions of the Old Testament, before Jerome's time, were translated from the Septuagint. It was a literary undertaking of the first degree of importance, when Jerome set himself to translate the Old Testament scriptures anew from the original language. And it was of the highest religious importance, since it was a setting aside of the Septuagintal tradition, and an assertion of the primary authority of the original language of the Scriptures.

It was an undertaking of almost equal literary and religious importance when Jerome set himself to revise the ancient Latin versions of the New Testament, of which there were several in circulation, and to produce a new version which should more exactly express the meaning of the original Greek.

Jerome brought to the great task a laborious diligence, a critical acumen, a competent learning, and a literary felicity, not unequal to the importance of the undertaking. In style, the translation is exceedingly pure, and bears testimony to the diligence with which he had studied the best Latin authors. No one can read the Vulgate without being struck by the contrast it presents in the classic simplicity of its language to the style of contemporary Latin writers, and even to the other writings of Jerome himself.

The version was not undertaken, as his early revision of the Gospels had been, with any ecclesiastical sanction, and it was not imposed upon the Church by any authority; it won its way by its intrinsic merits, and only slowly superseded the older versions. Augustine continued to use the old version to the end of his life. In the sixth century, the use of Jerome's version was universal among scholars, except in Africa, where the other still retained its ground. In the seventh century the traces of the old version grow rare. In the eighth century, though the old version was not forgotten, Jerome's version was everywhere that in ordinary use.

It is difficult to estimate the value of the service which Jerome thus conferred upon the Western Church. It will help some of our readers to appreciate the subject better if we compare the benefit which Jerome conferred upon Europe with that which Wiclif ·conferred upon England when he translated the whole Bible (mainly from Jerome's version) into the English tongue. Wiclif's was the Bible in the vulgar tongue of England, Jerome's was the Biblia Vulgata—the Bible in the vulgar tongue—of Europe; it continued to be the Bible of all Europe for eight centuries, and continues to be the Bible of the greater part of Europe to the present hour ; it is the basis of all the modern translations into the vernacular languages of Europe.

" But the Latin Bible, which thus passed gradually into use, under the name of Jerome, was a strangely composite work. The books of the Old Testament, with one exception, were certainly taken from his version from the Hebrew ; but this had not only been variously corrupted, but was in many particulars, especially in the Pentateuch, at variance with his later judgment. The Psalter, however, was retained from the old version, as Jerome had corrected it from the Septuagint. The Psalter was committed to memory by all ecclesiastics, and by many of the laity, and was constantly used in the services of the

Church, and it was found impossible, or at least inexpedient, to substitute the new and more correct version for it. We have a similar incident in the history of our own English version. When the Lessons, and the Epistles and Gospels in the Communion Service, were adopted into the Services of our Church from the present authorised version, it was found inexpedient to introduce the authorised version of the Psalter and Canticles into Liturgical use, and the Prayer Book still retains, and we still use every day, the confessedly less correct version of the Great Bible of 1540.[1]

In the New Testament, the text of the Gospels was in the main Jerome's revised edition; that of the remaining books his very incomplete revision of the old Latin.

Thus the present Vulgate contains elements which belong to every period and form of the Latin version.

(1.) *Unrevised Old Latin:* Wisdom, Ecclesiasticus, 1 and 2 Maccabees, and Baruch.

(2.) *Old Latin revised from the Septuagint :* the Psalter.

(3). *Jerome's free translation from the original text :* Judith, Tobit.

(4.) *Jerome's translation from the Original:* the Old Testament, except the Psalter.

---

[1] See note after the Preface to the Prayer-Book, respecting the order in which the Psalter is to be read :—"Note that the Psalter followeth the division of the Hebrews, and the translation of the Great English Bible set forth and used in the time of King Henry VIII. and Edward VI."

(5.) *Old Latin revised from Greek MSS.:* the Gospels.

(6.) *Old Latin cursorily revised:* the remainder of the New Testament."[1]

Gregory the Great, in the 6th century, while himself using Jerome's version, acknowledged that the old version was equally admitted by the Roman See.   It was not till the end of the sixteenth century that Pope Sixtus V., himself a scholar, produced an edition of the Vulgate, and "by the fulness of apostolic power decreed that this edition was to be received and held as true, lawful, authentic, and unquestioned, in all public and private discussion, reading, preaching, and explanation," and further enacted that the new revision should be introduced into all missals and service-books, and the greater excommunication threatened against all who in any way contravened the constitution.

This edition, however, had many faults, and a further revision was published in the pontificate of Clement VIII., in 1592, which is still the authorised edition of Jerome's work throughout the Roman Communion.

[1] Smith's "Dict. of the Bible," art. Vulgate.

CHAPTER XX.

THE ORIGENISTIC CONTROVERSY.

A.D. 395.

WE have seen that Hadrian's new city of Ælia Capitolina, through the constant presence of crowds of pilgrims from all parts of Christendom for a century past, had gradually grown into a great, wealthy, luxurious, and disorderly city.

It is a remarkable illustration of the principles on which the territorial divisions of the Church were organized, that Cæsarea, being the metropolis of the civil province of Palestine, had also been made the ecclesiastical metropolis, so that Jerusalem, the source of Christianity, and mother of all the Churches, was only a provincial Church, and its bishop a suffragan of the metropolitan of Cæsarea. The growing importance of Jerusalem, and the veneration in which it was held by Christendom, had made its bishops dissatisfied with their official status. They had, indeed, always enjoyed a certain undefined honour, which was recognized at the Council of Nicæa, on the ground of custom and ancient tradition. The bishop was, at this period, making the utmost of this *prestige*, was jealous of the legal superiority of Cæsarea, and was tentatively putting forth claims to independence, dignity, and jurisdiction, which a few years later were formally recognized, when the fourth General Council

allotted to the see the dignity of the Patriarchate, and
transferred to it the jurisdiction over the Churches of
Palestine, reserving to Cæsarea the honorary title of
Metropolitan. The present bishop, John, who had
succeeded the great Cyril in the year A.D. 386, when
not much more than thirty years of age, had some
reputation for learning, talent, and eloquence. The
Church of the Nativity at Bethlehem was under his
episcopal jurisdiction, and he had been the cordial
friend of the distinguished founders of the monasteries of Bethlehem.

Among the most distinguished members of the
Church of Jerusalem were Rufinus and Melania, who
had long resided in their monasteries on the Mount
of Olives, where Rufinus had made a reputation as
a man of letters,[1] and director of souls ; Melania was
known by the report of pilgrims for her high birth,
great wealth, and munificent charity.

Bethlehem was only six miles from Jerusalem, and
the recluses of the Cave of the Nativity were bound
by many ties, official and personal, to the holy city.

Though, perhaps, Jerome and Paula seldom quitted
their retirement to visit the holy city, and Rufinus
and Melania still more rarely visited Bethlehem, yet

---

[1] His chief works are an 'Historia Ecclesiastica,' in eleven
books, nine of which are loosely translated from Eusebius, the
other two being a continuation of the history to his own time ;
an 'Historia Eremitica,' being biographies of thirty-four of the
Nitrian hermits; an 'Expositio Symbolum'; his 'Apologia'
against Jerome, and numerous translations from the Greek.
He was a man of only moderate literary ability, and owes his
celebrity chiefly to his connection with Jerome.

we cannot doubt that there was a frequent communication between the friends by letter, and the constant flow of pilgrims direct from the guest-houses of the monasteries of Jerusalem to those of Bethlehem helped to maintain their intercourse. Unhappily, a religious controversy sprang up which ranged them on opposite sides, and led to a lamentable personal quarrel, which lasted for the rest of their lives. This was the controversy on the orthodoxy of 'Origen, which had agitated the Church during the lifetime of that great writer, had died away after his death, but now broke out once more, and threw the Church into confusion.

Origen was a man of undoubted piety, great learning, and brilliant genius. His writings contained much which was of great value ; but they also abounded in daring speculations, extending over the whole range of theological science. It was easy on one hand for scholars to have a high admiration of Origen's genius, and to use his writings with advantage ; and, on the other hand, it was equally easy to point out in his writings a large number of unorthodox speculations, and to condemn them as heretical and dangerous.

At this period, the latter was the received opinion in the Western Church, though the writings of Origen were little known there ; while, at the same time, in the Eastern Churches, Didymus, the blind master of the school of Alexandria, Basil of Cæsarea, Gregory Nazianzen, Gregory of Nyssa, and others, were his warm admirers.

John of Jerusalem, Rufinus and his monks, and Jerome and his friends, were among those who appreciated the value of Origen's writings ; Jerome had used his Hexapla as the standard text in his emendation of the Latin versions of the Bible, he had translated many of his homilies, in a preface to the translation of his homilies on the Song of Solomon he had given warm expression to his admiration of Origen, and he had made use of his works in his own expositions of Holy Scripture.

The controversy broke out again in Egypt, among the monks of the desert. The Nitrian monks were great admirers of Origen's mystical style ; others among the Egyptian recluses who took a narrow and literal view of divine things, were bitterly opposed to him. The latter class very generally fell into the error of anthropomorphism. Theophilus, in one of the Paschal Letters, which it was his duty yearly to issue, as Bishop of Alexandria, took the opportunity of denouncing anthropomorphism. The monks who held these views rushed to Alexandria with the intention, as was supposed, of killing him. He, however, dexterously pacified them, condemned Origenism at their desire, and used their fanaticism, and the odium attached to the name of Origen, in furtherance of his own intrigues. Soon after (A.D. 401) he denounced the Nitrians, who had incurred his displeasure, to the governor of Egypt as insubordinate ; invaded their solitude with soldiers ; and with violence, and even bloodshed, drove about 300 of them out of their monasteries. About eighty of them fled to Palestine. Through the influence of Theophilus they were compelled to remove thence, and sought refuge at Constantinople, where Chrysostom.

having learned that they were men of good repute, gave them hospitality, though he declined to receive them into communion without the assent of their own archbishop.

We have a little anticipated the history, and must go back some six or seven years to the year A.D. 395, when the controversy extended to Palestine, and the personages of our history became involved in it.   In that year a certain theologian named Aterbius, who had set himself to denounce and oppose Origenism, came to Jerusalem, and denounced the bishop, Rufinus and Jerome, as Origenists, and the whole diocese of Jerusalem as tainted with his errors.   The bishop John did not condescend to reply to his denunciations.   Rufinus shut himself up in his monastery, and declined to see him, or to enter into controversy with him personally or by letter.   Jerome, always ready to rush into the lists against any antagonist, always jealous of his reputation for orthodoxy, wrote at once in his own justification.   He pointed out that he had only made use of Origen in a guarded way; and admitted that the great Alexandrian was obnoxious to the charges of unsoundness brought against him, with a readiness which was very displeasing to John and Rufinus, and others of his admirers.   The smouldering disagreement among the friends soon broke out into open discord.

Epiphanius, bishop of Salamis, who, we remember, took part in the Council of Rome, and was the guest of Paula during its continuance, whom Paula subsequently visited in Cyprus on her way to the East, came to Jerusalem, and, as usual, took up his resi-

dence with the Bishop.   The Bishop of Salamis was
now more than eighty years of age ; he had a great
reputation for learning and for holiness, so that he
was regarded as a saint, and miracles and prophecies
were popularly attributed to him.   On the morning
after his arrival, at John's request, Epiphanius preached
in the Church of the Holy Sepulchre to a great crowd
of people, attracted by his reputation.   He directed
his discourse against Origenism and its abettors, and
every one felt that it was a direct attack upon John,
Rufinus, and the clergy of the diocese generally ; the
bishop expressed his impatience by looks and ges-
tures, and at length sent his archdeacon to bid the
preacher cease.   On leaving the church the people
pressed round Epiphanius.   They kissed his feet,
they tore off the fringe of his garments for relics,
women begged his blessing on their children.   John
angrily bade them make way, and accused Epiphanius
of encouraging the superstitious extravagance of the
people.

In the afternoon another sermon had been announced in the Church of the Holy Cross.   John
himself ascended the pulpit and preached against
Anthropomorphism, the error common among the
extreme opponents of Origen, manifestly intending
his sermon as a retort on Epiphanius's attack of the
morning.   When he had concluded his sermon
Epiphanius rose in his place and calmly said, that
all that John, his brother in the priesthood, and his
son in age, had said against the heresy of the Anthro-
pomorphites was well said, and he added his testimony to that of his brother against these heretics ;

but he said, as we both condemn this absurd error on
one extreme, so it is right that we should also both
condemn the perverse dogmas of Origen on the
other.   A general smile, followed by a burst of
applause, welcomed these words of the venerable
bishop, and it was felt that John had come off only
second best in the encounter.   Two days after John
embraced another opportunity to put himself right in
the estimation of his people and of the Church at
large.   It was Easter, and John recapitulated in his
sermon his teaching during Lent, which no doubt
had consisted of the usual catechetical lectures to
those about to be baptized on the festival, and took
occasion to make a careful doctrinal statement on
each of the great points of the Creed.   Then he
turned to Epiphanius and appealed to him whether
this declaration of faith was orthodox or not.   Epiphanius, thus appealed to, replied that he had nothing
to say against the doctrines which had been stated.
But when he had had time to think over what had
been said, it seemed to him that the statements of
John involved several errors, and that he had been
surprised into an unwarranted admission of his orthodoxy.   He quitted Jerusalem in anger without taking
leave of any one, went down to Bethlehem, recounted
to his friends there all that had taken place, and declared that henceforth he would hold no further communion with the heretical bishop.   The communities
of Bethlehem endeavoured to avert such a breach of
charity, but Epiphanius retired to his monastery of
Vetus Ad, in the diocese of Eleutheropolis, and
thence addressed a circular letter to all the monasteries

of Palestine, calling upon them to break off communion
with John if he did not speedily give satisfactory as-
surances of his orthodoxy.

The action of Epiphanius occasioned an open rup-
ture between the communities of Jerusalem and of
Bethlehem. Rufinus and Melania took part with the
bishop, Jerome and Paula with Epiphanius. John
directed the priests who served the Church of the
Nativity to refuse communion to Jerome and Paula
and their monks and nuns, and even to refuse them
admittance within the church and its precincts.
Jerome and Vincentius had both been ordained
priests, but had both abstained from the performance
of the duties of the office, and would not assume
them under the present circumstances; but Epiphanius, who had involved them in their difficulty,
took steps to meet its consequences. Paulinian,
Jerome's brother, now about twenty-eight years of
age, came to Epiphanius's monastery of Vetus Ad on
some business, and Epiphanius, acting as the bishops
of the time not unfrequently did, forced ordination
upon him without his consent, and then sent him to
minister to the communities of Bethlehem. John
retorted by uttering a formal excommunication against
all who accepted Paulinian as rightly ordained, and
as many of the townspeople of Bethlehem adhered to
the cause of their monastic neighbours, the interdict
included them.

Not satisfied with using all the ecclesiastical weapons
which he wielded, John sought to crush Jerome by
the weight of the civil power. Rufinus, the able but
corrupt and cruel minister of the latter part of

Theodosius's reign, still ruled the State under the young emperor Arcadius. To him the Bishop of Jerusalem addressed himself and obtained from him an order to the Count of Palestine for the exile of Jerome. It was a critical moment in Jerome's life; banishment under Rufinus usually meant a lingering death. But before the order could be executed,[1] the swords of the soldiers of Gainas had delivered the empire from the tyranny which had so long oppressed it. The Count of Cæsarea did not execute the order of the dead minister; John did not seek a renewal of it from the new favourite Eutropius; and Jerome remained unmolested in his cell. But the controversy was carried on with great bitterness between Rufinus of Jerusalem and Jerome. Each wrote and published his statement of the case in order to secure the sympathies of the Church, and each assailed the other with the fiercest personalities. A few sentences from Jerome's letters to Pammachius on the subject will suffice to show the tone of his treatment of the controversy.[2]

" It is we, forsooth, who divide the Church, and not you—you, who refuse a roof to the living, a grave to the dead, who seek the exile of your brethren! Who was it, then, who sought to excite against our lives that powerful wild beast who threatened the lives of all the world? Who commanded that the bones of the saints—their unoffending ashes—should be de-

---

[1] The wife and daughter of Rufinus were banished to Jerusalem. His sister, Sylvia, was a Church virgin, and celebrated for her saintliness.

[2] Ep. xxxviii.

prived of burial, buffeted by wind and rain, and exposed to all the outrages of the weather? These are the gentle caresses with which the good shepherd wooes us to peace, and paternally reproaches us with wishing to withdraw ourselves from his authority.

"But we do not heed it; we are not in schism; we are united in the communion of charity with all the bishops who possess the true faith. Do you alone constitute the Church; and he who offends you, or whom you do not like, is he necessarily cut off from Christ? If you assert your episcopal authority over us, act as a bishop to us, and not as a persecutor. That which separates between us and you is a question of the faith. We said it before, and we repeat it: Prove to us that you are a Christian, that you are a Catholic, and there will remain no other question of difference between us except the ordination of Paulinian.

"Your complaints on that subject are based on very fine reasons. You object to Paulinian's age; but you ordain a priest and send him as your legate and associate, and while you untruly call Paulinian a boy, you send a boy-priest to say so.

"Paulinian, you say, was ordained in your diocese without your consent. But did not you bring the deacon Theosebius from the Church of Tyre to make him a priest of Bethlehem because he is our enemy, because you think him eloquent, and because you wish to see him overwhelm us with his thunders? You can tread under foot all the canons because all your caprices are rights, all your acts are rules of faith. You dare to cite the venerable Epiphanius

before the tribunal of Christ to be judged there with
you! You reproach the holy bishop with the hospitality of your roof and the fellowship of your table;
and you wrote that before the discourse in the Church
of the Holy Sepulchre he had never spoken to you
about Origen, nor about his doubts of your orthodoxy. You wrote that; you took God to witness the
truth of the statement. Epiphanius, however, affirms
the contrary. Not only has he written it, but he has
said it to your face; he has said it to all the world;
he has said it to us in presence of our whole congregation, which is ready to bear witness to it. . . .
But I stop; for the honour of the episcopate I am
unwilling to convict a bishop of perjury."

Archelaus, the count of Palestine, tried to bring
about a reconciliation, and came to Bethlehem to
mediate between the two parties, but John made
excuses for absenting himself. He, however, also
sought intervention, writing complaints to Alexandria
and to Rome. Theophilus of Alexandria, who was
ambitious and domineering, and at that time a sup-
porter of the Origenist party, listened to John's
request, and undertook to judge the dispute, though
he had no ecclesiastical right to interfere in the
affairs of the Church of Palestine.

Jerome protested against this interference as a
breach of ecclesiastical order. "Behold," he says,
"the loyalty of this bishop, who invokes as judge of
a dispute the man who is the author of it. See his
obedience to the laws of the Church, who, on a
question involving discipline as well as dogma, invokes a foreign tribunal. Has Cæsarea then ceased

to exist; is it no longer the metropolis of Palestine?
Has the Church of Jerusalem been transferred under
the jurisdiction of Alexandria?"[1]

Theophilus sent Isidore[2] as his representative.
The legate was preceded by two letters from Theophilus, one to the Bishop of Jerusalem, the other to
Vincentius of Bethlehem; and by one of those
dramatic errors which sometimes do happen in real
life, the letters were missent. That intended for
John fell into the hands of the community of Bethlehem, and showed them that the case was prejudged
against them. When Isidore came to Bethlehem
Jerome attempted to argue the question of John's
orthodoxy. Isidore refused to enter into the matter,
and held him to this dilemma : "You communicated
with John, therefore, if he is a heretic, so are you, or
else you accuse him falsely of being a heretic, and
you are a calumniator."

In vain Jerome replied, "That when he communicated with him he was ignorant of his unorthodoxy,
perhaps, indeed, at that time he was orthodox; but
when the letters of Epiphanius had made him aware
that John was unsound in the faith, then he refused
to communicate with him."

But before Isidore had come to any conclusion in
the matter, Theophilus suddenly changed his policy.
He had become hostile to the Origenist party in his
own province, and commenced a persecution against
them. Some of the Nitrian monks of this party,

---

[1] Ep. xxxviii.

[2] The same who had visited Rome with Athanasius, see p. 21,
and had been their host at Alexandria, see p. 131.

whom he had excommunicated, were also, at his instance, exiled by the Prefect of Egypt to Palestine, and Theophilus hastened to move against them the leaders of the anti-Origenist party in Palestine. He addressed letters to Epiphanius and Jerome, congratulating them on their soundness in the faith, and asking their help in putting down the impious sect! John, thus thrown over, made overtures of reconciliation, which Jerome accepted ; the interdict upon his monasteries and his adherents was at once removed, and Paulinian's ordination was recognized by the bishop. Not only so, but John offered, and Jerome accepted, the direction of the Church of the Nativity. A reconciliation was also effected between Rufinus and Jerome ; the bishop celebrated the Holy Communion in the Church of the Resurrection, and Jerome and Rufinus took one another's hands over the Saviour's tomb in token of reconciliation, and confirmed it by receiving the pledges of charity together.

Jerome threw himself heartily into the controversy, overwhelmed Theophilus with praises, and translated into Latin three of his Paschal letters against Origen, with other documents relating to the controversy. Epiphanius, at the request of the Bishop of Alexandria, held a synod of his Cypriot bishops, who condemned the works of Origen, and Epiphanius wrote to Chrysostom to urge him to take a similar action ; and as Chrysostom took no step in the matter, he himself proceeded to Constantinople. He refused Chrysostom's offer of hospitality, and protested that he would hold no communication with him, unless he

o

consented to condemn Origen, and expelled the Nitrian refugees. Chrysostom replied that he left both Origen and the refugees to the judgment of a council which had been summoned. Epiphanius, however, became aware that the merits of the case were not quite as Theophilus had represented them, and, without waiting for the Synod, he returned to his own island.

We must not do more than allude to the factious synod, chiefly of Egyptian bishops, which Theophilus assembled at the oak near Chalcedon, under the patronage of the Court; to the condemnation and banishment of Chrysostom; and to his death in exile. We have only to say, with regret, that Jerome was, through all these transactions, of the party of the opponents of the Golden-mouthed Preacher, and translated into Latin a "brutal book,"[1] which, after his banishment, Theophilus wrote against him. We will hope that he also concurred in the subsequent reversal of the condemnation of Chrysostom, and the general regret for the undeserved persecution of one of the greatest of the bishops of the Catholic Church.

Robertson's 'History of the Christian Church.'

CHAPTER XXI.

The Visit of Fabiola.

A.D. 395.

It must not be supposed that the recluses of Bethlehem were as much out of the way of the world as similar persons would be now in the same locality. The facilities of travel were very considerable. The principal countries of the civilized world were situated round the Mediterranean Sea, the principal cities were on its shores ; its waters afforded a great highway from one country to another, Roman roads connected the seaports with the inland cities, and the postal service was well conducted. But what especially made travelling safe and easy was that all the countries were under one strong government, Greek or Latin was spoken by the educated and commercial classes everywhere, and the same habits and customs obtained in every city. The traveller visited Europe, Africa, and Asia, and was nowhere in a foreign country, but everywhere a Roman among Romans, for all the civilized world was Roman. It is interesting to observe how cosmopolitan people were. We need not go beyond the pages of this history for illustrations. Jerome, born in Venetia, is sent to Rome as to a university ; afterwards studies at Treves ; migrates to Antioch ; becomes a recluse in Chalcis ; spends three years in Constantinople ;

O 2

then returns to Rome; visits Egypt; and spends the
rest of his days in Palestine. Rufinus was a monk of
Aquileia; he settles on the Mount of Olives; and
returns (we shall see presently) to live in his country
house near his native city. Epiphanius, of Jewish
race, born in Palestine, builds a monastery at Eleutheropolis, in his native province, removes to Cyprus,
and builds monasteries there, is elected bishop of its
principal city, and still continues to rule his Syrian
monastery, and occasionally to reside there. Basil, a
Cappadocian, educated at Athens, is Bishop of
Cæsarea; Gregory of Nazianzum, Bishop of Constantinople; Chrysostom is transferred from the
priesthood in Antioch to the episcopate in Constantinople. Augustine, a native of Numidia, educated
at Carthage, teaches rhetoric at Rome, then takes a
professorship at Milan, is ordained priest at Hippo,
and elected to the bishopric of that See.

Travelling being so safe and easy, people travelled
a great deal, some on affairs of state, some on commercial affairs, some on affairs of the Church and of
religion. There were vast numbers of pilgrims, every
season, to the holy places of Palestine; every one who
visited the holy places visited the Cradle of the Nativity; and of all the pilgrims who visited Bethlehem a
great number were the guests of the monasteries
there. Indeed, Jerome and Paula, — the most
famous scholar of the Church, in his grotto cell,
and the daughter of the Scipios, in her nun's habit,
—were now visited with as much interest as that
with which they themselves had visited the hermit
fathers of the Egyptian desert in former years. Thus

a constant stream of visitors from all parts of the world passed through the guest houses of Bethlehem, and kept the inmates of the monasteries *au courant* with the world.

Among other visitors, about the year 395, Fabiola came unexpectedly, accompanied by Oceanus. We have already seen that these two were members of the ascetic party in Rome, during Jerome's residence there in the time of Bishop Damasus. Fabiola, a daughter of the great Fabian house, had had the misfortune to be married in very early youth to a husband who so ill-treated her that she was driven to rescue herself out of his hands by the method, which was only too common among the Roman aristocracy, of a divorce. Soon she contracted another marriage, which turned out still more unhappy than the first, and she quitted her second husband without seeking a formal divorce. During this troubled time of her early life she had sought the consolations of religion in the society of the religious ladies who frequented the palace of Marcella on the Aventine. These religious impressions had gradually grown in strength, and at length had impelled her to visit the Holy Land, partly, like others, to make the customary pilgrimage of the holy places, partly to consult Jerome on a case of conscience which troubled her. Paula, Eustochium, and Jerome received their friends Fabiola and Oceanus with delight ; Fabiola took up her residence with her friends in their monastery, Oceanus his in the monastery of Jerome, and both entered heartily into the holy life and learned pursuits of the place.

While these Roman guests were with them, the

tranquil life of Bethlehem was interrupted by a flash
and thunder-peal from the great storm which was
gathering from the North and East about the Roman
Empire, and which was shortly to shatter it into ruins.
The Huns had passed the barrier of the Caucasus,
they were besieging Antioch, they were marching on
Jerusalem.[1] City after city, unwarlike and defenceless, fell before their horsemen ; fire and massacre
plunder and rapine, marked their rapid progress.
Jerome took immediate steps to save the lives of his
monks, and the honour of Paula's nuns. He took
them all down to the sea-coast, and established them
in a temporary camp; he hired ships, and kept them
ready, to embark the whole company on the approach
of the foe, and seek safety in flight.

As it turned out, the barbarian hordes returned
upon their steps before they had crossed the Lebanon,
and Jerome and Paula, and their flocks, returned with
Alleluias to their homes in Bethlehem.

Fabiola, however, resolved not to return to Bethlehem, but to embark at once for Rome, Oceanus
being still the protector of her return. She had not
propounded her case of conscience to Jerome in
person; but Amandus, a priest of her company,
wrote to Jerome, asking the solution of some theological questions, and he enclosed Fabiola's case as
if it were the case of his own sister. The case,
as proposed, was this. If a woman has left her husband on account of adultery and other crimes, and
has taken a second husband through force (*per*

---

[1] Ep. lxxxiv.

vim), can she, without penitence, be in communion with the Church, the first husband being still alive. Jerome saw that the case thus put in the name of another person, was the case of Fabiola, and, while allowing the question to remain under the pseudonym, he was careful to make his reply meet the real facts of Fabiola's case. He declared that, according to the law of the Church, while her first husband lived, she could not have a second. The assertion that she had taken the second husband *per vim*, called forth some severe, but apparently well-deserved, remarks. "When I read it, I called to mind that verse : *ad excusandas excusationes in peccatis* (Ps. 140). We all favour our own vices, and what we have done of our own will we attribute to the necessity of nature. How, if a youth say : I suffer violence from my body, desire drives me to lust? And again, if a homicide says : I was in need, I wanted food, I had no covering for my body, I shed blood lest I should die of hunger and cold? Therefore reply to your sister, who asks me about her state, not mine but the Apostle's sentence : ' Know ye not, brethren, for I speak to them that know the law, how that the law hath dominion over a man as long as he liveth. For the woman is bound by the law to her husband so long as he liveth. But if he is dead she is free from that law, so that, while her husband liveth, she is an adulteress if she be married to another man.' Therefore," he concludes, " if your sister wishes to receive Christ's Body, and not to be reckoned an adulteress, let her do penance."[1]

---

[1] Ep. lxv. ad Amandum.

Fabiola, receiving this letter soon after her return
to Rome, accepted the decision, and determined
to act upon it, and do public penance for the sin
which she had committed. Six years before, the great
Emperor Theodosius had consented, at the injunction
of Ambrose, to do public penance at Milan for the
massacre at Thessalonica ; the Roman patriciate was
now scandalized, or edified, according to their view of
the transaction, by the spectacle of the daughter
of the Fabii on the steps of the Lateran Church,
in mourning habit, with dishevelled hair, sprinkled
with ashes, among the other sinners who sought there
formal absolution, and readmission to the privileges of
a Christian. Jerome points out the significance of the
event.   The civil law of Rome allowed the right
of divorce and remarriage, the practice was common ;
the public penance of Fabiola emphasized the view
that " the laws of Cæsar were one thing, the laws
of Christ another," and that the laws of Christ take
precedence among Christians.

The sequel of the life of Fabiola was in accordance
with this act. She renounced the world, sold her
property, built hospitals, and ministered with her own
hands to the sick and poor.

CHAPTER XXII.

THE APOLOGIA IN RUFINUM.

A.D. 395-404.

THE reconciliation between Jerome and Rufinus was only a patched-up truce, and the quarrel soon broke out again with greater violence, the scene being transferred from Palestine to Rome.

Soon after the restoration of communion between John of Jerusalem and the communities of Bethlehem, Rufinus had quitted Jerusalem, and returned to live in Rome. Here, at the request of a student named Macarius, he undertook a translation of one of Origen's works, the "Peri Archôn," which was at once the most famous and the most unorthodox. But in translating it, Rufinus modified some of its most objectionable passages, both by omission and addition, so as to give the work a more orthodox tone. To this translation Rufinus prefixed a preface, in which he endeavoured to disarm criticism by paying many compliments to the learning and orthodoxy of Jerome, and quoting Jerome's eulogy of Origen in the preface to his translation of the homilies on the Song of Solomon. In his teaching and conversation Rufinus seems to have pursued a similar plan, supporting his own Origenistic teaching by reference to the works of Jerome, in which he had made use of the Alexandrian father. The friends of Jerome were perplexed. The representation of Origen's opinions, thus published to the Latin world, seemed not to justify the condemnation which the Latin Church had uttered against them, and the use which Rufinus made of Jerome's name seemed to place him among the Origenists.

Jerome replied by preparing an exact translation of the work "Peri Archôn," which Rufinus had thus tampered with, and sending it to Rome, with a preface in the shape of a letter to Pammachius and Marcella, in which he indignantly repels the specious compliments which Rufinus had paid him.

The Origenistic controversy deeply agitated the Roman Church. Siricius, the bishop, was satisfied of Rufinus's orthodoxy, but on his death his successor, Anastasius, summoned Rufinus, who had removed to Milan, to explain his conduct, and to give satisfactory evidences of his orthodoxy. Rufinus contented himself with sending a written defence, and withdrew to his native place, Aquileia, where he had an estate, and where the bishop Chromatius was his personal friend. Anastasius called together a synod, which anathematized Origen and the upholders of his errors, and indirectly censured Rufinus; an Egyptian synod also had just condemned Origen; and these synodical decisions concluded the controversy.

Rufinus, during the next three years, wrote an elaborate defence or "Apologia," which was also an elaborate attack upon Jerome. Jerome replied with another Apologia, which was also an eloquent defence of himself, and at the same time a violent attack upon Rufinus. Rufinus certainly employed all his skill in

tearing the character of Jerome to pieces.   Jerome
replied with a virulence and coarseness the more
offensive from contrast with the hyperbolical praises
he had formerly lavished on his friend.   We are re-
minded of the controversy between Milton and
Salmasius.   We will only give one example of the
tone of this lamentable polemic.   The reader will
remember the vision which St. Jerome saw in his cell
in Chalcis, in which he suffered the scourge for
having given his time and talents to the heathen
authors, and swore never to read a profane book
again.   Rufinus recalls this story, and accuses Jerome
of perjury, since he did subsequently read heathen
books, frequently quoted the heathen classics in his
writings, and taught them to the youth of Bethlehem,
having engaged Rufinus's monks to make copies of
them for his use.   Jerome replies :[1] "This is
assuredly a mode of attack the glory of whose inven-
tion belongs to you only, to accuse me on account of
a dream.   You love me so much as to be uneasy
even about my dreams.   Take care, however, for the
voice of the prophet warns us not to put faith in
dreams.   If I dream about an adultery, that will not
cast me into hell, nor if I dream of the crown of
martyrdom will that raise me up to heaven."   Wherein
is an allusion whose meaning will presently appear.
" Yes, I confess it, I often dream.   How often have
I dreamed that I saw myself dead, and laid in my
grave.   How often have I seemed to fly above the
earth, and cross mountains and seas in my flight.

[1] In Rufin. L.

Am I then obliged to live no longer? or ought I, at your demand, to fix feathers on my shoulders and sides, because my mind, like that of other mortals, mocks itself with empty dreams? How many men, rich in their dreams, awake in poverty? How many thirsting, drink rivers in their sleep, and wake up with burning throat? Such is other people's case, and such is also mine; and I demand that I should not be held accountable for promises which I may have made in my dreams. But let us speak seriously, and coming back to realities, let us occupy ourselves with what we ought to do when awake. Have you kept all which you promised in your baptism? Yes, we two, who are monks; have we examined whether, skilful in seeing the mote in our neighbour's eye, we have cast out the beam from our own? I say it with sincere grief, it is not good, it is contrary to the law of God, to call a man your friend, to load him with praises, and then to persecute him, not only in his real life, but even into his dreams, and to make what he has said or done in his dreams a subject of attack." Rufinus was accustomed to boast that he had suffered for the faith in Alexandria, no one knew on what occasion. Jerome continues in allusion to this: " You, also, my brother, dream sometimes, you see yourself in your sleep a prisoner of the Lord, you fancy yourself snatched from the jaws of a lion, you fancy yourself fighting with wild beasts in the circus of Alexandria, and when you awake, you exclaim with pride, ' I have finished my course, I have kept the faith, there remains for me a crown of righteousness.' Calm yourself, and consider, and you will see that this is only a dream like mine.   A man is not a confessor without a prison, he is not exiled without a decree of banishment.   Can you tell us where your prison was situated ?   Can you tell the names of your judges ? Try to remember, for no one has ever heard anything of it either in Egypt or elsewhere.   Produce the record of your examination, and among the acts of the rest of the Alexandrian martyrs we shall recite yours also, and you may say to those who assail you, ' I bear in my body the marks of the Lord Jesus.' "[1] In writing to others, Jerome expressed contempt of his antagonist's learning and eloquence, threw out insinuations against his moral character, condescended to ridicule his personal appearance and little tricks of habit.   After his usual custom, he fitted him with a nickname : Marcus Grunnius Corocotta Porcellus was the burlesque name of the hero of a farce popular in Rome at the moment ; and since Rufinus had a trick, not uncommon with public speakers, of making a little inarticulate noise at the beginning of his sentences, Jerome fastened upon him the vulgar name of Grunnius—the grunter.   And thus these two quondam friends, these two learned doctors, these two Christian men, brought to bear all their rhetorical skill to injure one another's reputation, while judicious friends tried to mediate in vain, and the whole Church was scandalized at the quarrel.

With this polemic with Rufinus was mixed up another with Vigilantius.   This was a priest from the Western part of Gaul, who had brought letters of

---

[1] In Rufin. iii.

introduction to Jerome, remained some time as his guest at Bethlehem, and on his return to Europe had published two essays. In one essay he attacked Jerome and his friends, declared them all Origenists, and asserted that in personal discussion he had reduced Jerome to silence. In a second essay he wrote against those ascetic doctrines of which Jerome was the special champion. He attacked the exaltation of virginity and mortification, and the reverence paid to saints, and the like. Jerome seasons his reply with his usual vigorous and coarse personalities. With his happy knack at giving nicknames, instead of Vigilantius (watchful) he fastens on his antagonist the name of Dormitantius (sleepy). He rakes up a story that the father of "Dormitantius" was an innkeeper, and taunts him with it, with the skill and ferocity of a gladiator, who is bruising and crushing a combatant of inferior strength with blows of his iron-bound cestus :—

"Brother," he writes to him, "return to the calling you followed in your youth. It is not good to change thus. It is one thing to have a taste for wines, and another to understand the Prophets and Apostles, one thing to be clever at detecting bad shillings, and another to be a judge of texts of Scripture. I shall not accuse the venerable Paulinus of having deceived me in introducing you into my house, for I was deceived myself; for I mistook your rusticity for a modest humility. Still, if you are determined to be a doctor, take a friend's advice—go to school ; attend the lectures of the grammarians and rhetoricians ; study dialectics ; inform yourself as to the opinions of the philosophers; and when you have done all that, then—learn to hold your tongue! I am afraid, however that it is waste of time to give you advice, you who offer advice to everybody; I should do better to call to mind the Greek proverb, 'Don't play the lyre to an ass!'"

Two letters written about this time contain some notices of the Christian customs of the age, which are interesting.   One is upon the death of Nepotian. Nepotian was the nephew of Heliodorus, the friend of Jerome's youth, to whom he wrote his praise of the eremitical life, and who had been consecrated Bishop of Altinum.   Nepotian had, like his uncle, been an officer in the army, and one of the Imperial Guard.   But in the palace of the Cæsar he had led an ascetic life; beneath the gilded breastplate he had worn hair-cloth, and at length he had proposed to retire from the world and become a monk.   His uncle, however, begged him to aid him in the duties of his church.   Jerome was appealed to; and, calling to mind the exhortations which Jerome had addressed to Heliodorus in former years, bidding him break all family ties, and step over the body of his father, to follow his ascetic vocation, it is a pleasant surprise to find him now exhorting Nepotian to yield to his uncle's wishes, and pointing out how he could combine the principles of the ascetic life with the duties of the secular priesthood.   When the young man lay on his death-bed (396 A.D.) he sent to Jerome, as a token of affection, the alb (tunic) which he had assumed by his advice.   Jerome gave utterance to his own grief, and endeavoured to con-

sole his friend in a long and charming letter. Certainly the warmth and tenderness of his friendships
equal the bitterness of his enmities, and help us to
do justice to the sensitiveness of feeling out of which
both spring, and reconcile us to the great passionate
soul, alternately thrilling with indignation and melting
into tears.

CHAPTER XXIII.

THE DEATH OF PAULA.

A.D. 397-403.

In the year 397 A.D. a heavy blow fell upon the heads of the whole community of Bethlehem in the death of Paulina, Paula's third daughter, in childbirth of her first child, which also died with her. She left her wealth to her husband Pammachius, with the condition that he should distribute it among the poor. He did more than fulfil her bequest; he added a portion of his own wealth to hers. It was an ancient custom among the Greeks and Romans to make a great feast and distribute presents over the tombs of their illustrious dead. The Church had adopted the custom in the feasts which were celebrated at the tombs of the martyrs on the vigils of their commemoration days. Pammachius observed the custom in honour of his dead wife. He caused it to be proclaimed by sound of trumpet throughout Rome that a funeral feast, followed by a distribution of money, would be made to the poor in the Church of St. Peter at the funeral of Paulina. Crowds assembled. Pammachius himself presided. The long tables spread in the church were filled again and again with guests. As they departed Pammachius gave to each a new robe and a considerable alms. "Some

P

husbands," says Jerome, " assuage their grief by
scattering upon the tombs of their wives violets, roses,
lilies, and purple flowers; Pammachius bedews this
holy dust with the balm of charity." Pammachius
became a monk. It is a striking picture which is
placed before us when we are told that he took his
place in the Senate in his brown monk's tunic, amidst
the laughter of his pagan colleagues.

One ray of gladness illumines the gathering gloom
of these latter years of our history. Toxotius, the son
of Paula, and heir of the honours and wealth of so
great a house, had been married in his fourteenth
year to Leta, the daughter of Albinus. Though
Albinus was a pagan and a Pontiff of the pagan gods,
yet he held his hereditary religion with the laxity of
a philosophical incredulity. His wife had been a
Christian ; he had allowed her to bring up her
daughters Christians; he had married them to pagan
or Christian husbands indifferently. Toxotius was
shortly converted by the influence of his Christian
wife. Leta, for some time childless, had made a vow
that if God would give her a daughter, she would
devote her to a religious life. A daughter was born
to them, and they fulfilled their promise. The child
was named Paula after her grandmother.

Jerome, in his letter of congratulation, draws a
charming picture of the Pontiff of the gods surrounded by his Christian children and grandchildren,
with the newly-born on his knees, listening with
pleasure to her first attempts to lisp the Alleluia, which
was the first word her mother taught her. Jerome
foresaw the possibility that these sweet influences

would even lead the aged Pontiff to èmbrace the
Faith; at least with admirable skill he seized the
occasion to throw out a suggestion, which he knew
would be zealously followed up: "How a holy and
believing house," he wrote to Leta, "sanctifies the
unbelieving. Albinus is already a candidate for
Christianity, a crowd of Christian children and grandchildren lay siege to him. For my part, I believe if
Jupiter himself had such a family, he would be converted to Jesus Christ. Let the Pontiff laugh and
ridicule my letter, let him call me stupid or mad, I
give him leave; his son-in-law Toxotius did so before
his conversion; one becomes, one is not born, a
Christian. The capitol and its gilded ceilings are
neglected, soot and cobwebs clothe the temples of
Rome; the city removes from its foundations and
takes up new ground; and its people pass like a
torrent by the ruined chapels of the gods to resort
to the tombs of the martyrs."[1]

The happy mother wrote to ask Jerome's advice as
to the bringing-up of her little devotee, and Jerome
replied with an elaborate essay; and if we smile when
we find the aged scholar directing that an alphabet
should be written on pieces of ivory and given to the
child for playthings, and she should be taught to recognise the forms of the letters and tell their names,
and that they should now and then be shuffled
together, and she should name them as they happen
to come; yet, as we continue to read, we become
interested in the ideal which he draws of the educa-

Ep. lvii.

P 2

tion and training of a Christian soul. But he begged
the mother to send the child to Bethlehem, where
her grandmother Paula, and her aunt Eustochium,
and he himself, would " form the heart of the young
spouse of Christ."

But the clouds threatened again. Soon after
Paulina's death Rufina also died. Then Paula's
health, undermined by years of excessive austerities,
gave way; and towards the end of the year 403 she
took to her bed, never to quit it again. Jerome
describes her sickness and death.[1]

"§ 27. In Paula's last sickness, her daughter 'would
be sitting upon the bed's side; she would wave the
fan; she would hold up her head, shake up the
pillow, rub her feet, cherish her stomach with her
hand, compose her bed, warm water for her, bring
the basin, and anticipate all the maids in these services,
and what any other did, she held that she herself
lost so much of her reward. With what prayers,
lamentations, and groanings, she would hasten up
and down between the cave of the Lord and her
mother lying in her bed, praying that she might not
be deprived of her companionship, that she might
not live an hour after her, that the same bier might
bear them both to the grave . . . .

"§ 28. Why do I make any further delay, and
increase my sorrow by prolonging it? This most wise
of women felt that death was at hand, part of her body
and her limbs being already cold; there was only a
little warmth of life which weakly breathed in her holy

---

[1] Ep. ad Eustochium.

breast, and yet, as if she were going to visit friends,
and take leave of strangers, she murmured those verses :
'O Lord, I have loved the beautiful order of Thy house,
and the place of the habitation of Thy glory,' and
' How lovely are Thy tabernacles, O God of power,
my soul hath even fainted with the desire of entering
into the court of Thy house,' and ' I have chosen
to be an abject in the house of my God rather than
to dwell in the tabernacles of sinners.'   And when I
asked her why she was silent, and would not answer
us, and whether she was in any pain, she answered
me in Greek, that ' she had no trouble, but that she
saw all things before her in tranquillity and peace.'
After this she was silent, and shutting her eyes, as
one who now despised mortal things, she repeated
these verses so that we could hardly hear what she
said, even till she breathed out her soul, and applying
her finger to her mouth, she made the sign of the
cross upon her lips.   Her spirit fainted, and panted
apace towards death ; and her soul even longing to
break out, she converted the very rattling of her
throat, wherewith mortal creatures use to end their
life, into the praises of our Lord.   There were
present the bishops of Jerusalem and other cities,
and an innumerable multitude of priests of inferior
rank, and Levites.   The whole monastery was filled
with choirs of virgins and monks . . . .

"§ 29. From the moment of her death forward
there was no lamentation nor doleful cry, as is wont
to be upon the death of men of this world, but there
were whole troops of people who chanted out the
Psalms in different tongues.   Paula's body was carried

to the tomb by the hands of bishops, who bent their
necks under the bier, whilst other bishops carried
lamps and tapers before the body; others led the
choirs of singers; and she was laid in the middle of
her Church of the Nativity of our blessed Saviour.
The whole crowd of the cities of Palestine came to
her funeral. Which of the monks hidden in the
wilderness remained in his cell? Which of the virgins
was hidden by the most secret chamber? He thought
that he committed sacrilege who omitted to pay the
last office to such a creature. The widows and the
poor, after the example of Dorcas, showed the clothes
which she had given them. The whole multitude
of needy people cried out that they had lost their
mother and their nurse. What is strange, the pale-
ness of death had not changed her face at all, but a
certain dignity and gravity did so possess her countenance, that you would not have thought her dead
but sleeping. The Psalms were sung in order, in
Hebrew, Greek, Latin, and Syriac, not only for those
three days till her body was buried, under the church
and near the cave of our Lord, but during the whole
week, all they who came in did the like, believing
best in those funerals which themselves made, and in
their own tears. The venerable virgin, her daughter
Eustochium, like an infant weaned from her nurse,
could scarce be drawn from her mother. She kissed
her eyes, and clung to her face, and embraced her
whole body, and even would have been buried with
her mother.

"§ 30. I take Jesus to witness, that she left not
a single coin to her daughter, but she left her

deeply in debt, and (which is yet matter of more difficulty) an immense number of brothers and sisters, whom it was hard to feed, and impious to put away."

Jerome himself was overwhelmed with sorrow. Some months afterwards, he writes to Theophilus of Alexandria, in reply to an inquiry about some literary work he had asked of him, that he had been so overcome with sadness, that he had not been able to pursue his usual tasks. But he made an effort, at the request of Eustochium, and for her consolation, to write a sketch of the life and character of Paula, from which the foregoing particulars are taken.

From the same source we intercalate a few sentences of his description of her character, and the concluding paragraph.

He begins: "§ 1. If my whole being were to become a tongue and voice, it would not suffice to proclaim worthily the virtues of the venerable Paula. Noble by her birth, more noble by her sanctity, powerful once through her wealth, more illustrious now for her poverty in Christ. The daughter of the Gracchi and the Scipios, the heir of Paulus Emilius, whose name she bore, the direct descendant of Marcia Papyria, the mother of Africanus, she preferred Bethlehem to Rome, and exchanged for a mud cottage the splendour of a palace. We do not weep that we have lost her, but we thank God that we once possessed her. What do I say! We possess her still, for all live by the Spirit of God, and the elect who ascend to Him still remain in the family of those who love them . . . .

" § 15. Now, let her virtue be described more at large, which is properly her own, and in describing which, God is judge and witness, I promise to add nothing, to exaggerate nothing, as is the manner of panegyrists, but to say less than I might on many points, lest I should exceed the truth, lest my detractors, who are always on the watch to set their sharp teeth in me, should suppose that I invent and adorn an Æsop's crow with borrowed plumes. In humility, which is the highest virtue of Christians, she so abased herself that any one who had not seen her before, and who desired to see her on account of her celebrity, would not have believed that it was she but the lowest of her maidens. And when she was surrounded by the thronging choirs of virgins, both in dress, and voice, and manner, and rank, she was the least of all. Never, from the death of her husband to the day of her own going to sleep, did she eat with any man, however holy, not even if he were of episcopal dignity. She never entered the bath unless she were sick ; even in a dangerous fever she used no soft beds, but rested upon the hard ground with scanty hair-cloth covering, if, indeed, that is to · be called rest which joined the days and nights together by almost continual prayers . . . .

" If among so many and great virtues I praise her chastity, I shall seem to be superfluous, for in that, while yet she lived in the world, she was the example of all the matrons of Rome, and lived so that even the voice of slander never dared to invent anything against her. There was nothing more kind than her disposition, nothing more gentle towards the lowly.

She did not court the powerful, nor did she fastidiously despise the proud and vain-glorious. If she saw a poor man she relieved him, if a rich man she exhorted him to charity. In liberality alone, she went beyond bounds, and while in debt, and paying interest, she would borrow more that she might not deny help to one who sought it. I confess my error. When she was too lavish in her liberality, I would oppose her with that saying of the Apostle, "Not that others be relieved by your being burdened, but by an equality, that at this time your abundance should help their want, and their abundance should help your want." And that text of the gospel of the Saviour, "He who hath two coats let him give one to him who has none." And that we should be prudent, and not give so liberally that we have nothing left to give : and much more in the same strain, which she with admirable modesty and sparing speech would parry, calling God to witness that she did everything for His sake, and that she earnestly desired that she might die a beggar, and not leave a single coin to her daughter, and at her death be indebted to charity for the shroud she was wrapped in. In conclusion, she would say, I, if I want to beg, can find many who will give to me, but this beggar, if he does not get from me what I can give him, though it be out of borrowed money, and if he should die, from whom will his life be required."

He concludes :—

" §. 32. I have dictated this book for you at two sittings-up, with the same grief which you yourself sustain. For, as often as I set myself to write, to perform the task which I had promised, so often did my fingers grow numb, my hand fell, my mind failed. Whence even my unpolished speech, so far from any elegance or conceit of words, doth witness well in what case the writer was.

"§. 33. Farewell, O Paula, and help thou by thy prayers the old age of him who bears thee a religious reverence. Thy faith and works have joined thee to Christ, and, being present with Him, thou wilt more easily obtain what thou desirest. ' I have raised to thee a monument more durable than brass,'[1] which no age will be able to destroy. I have cut an elogium upon thy sepulchre, which I have added at the foot of this volume, that, wheresoever my work shall come, the reader may understand that thou wert praised, and that thou art buried in Bethlehem."

(We append a quaint old metrical translation of the Epitaph.)

THE TITLE WRITTEN ON THE TOMB.

She whom the Paulos got, the Scipios bore,
The Gracchis, and great Agamemnon's race,
Lies here interred, called Paula heretofore—
Eustochium's mother, court of Rome's chief grace,
Seeks for Christ's poor and Bethlehem's rural face.

WRITTEN UPON THE FRONT OF THE GROT.

Seest thou, cut out of rock, this narrow tomb?
'Tis Paula's house, who now in heaven reigns;
And leaving brother, kindred, country, Rome,
Children, and wealth, in Bethlehem's grot remaynes.
Here is thy crib, O Christ; here, unprofaned,
The Magi presents brought to God human'd.

Horace, bk. iii. last Ode.

"§ 34. The holy and blessed Paula slept on the seventh of the kalends of February, on the Tuesday, after sunset. She was buried on the 5th of the kalends of the same month, Honorius Augustus for the sixth time, and Aristenetus for the first time, consuls. She lived in her holy resolution for five years at Rome, and twenty years at Bethlehem. She lived fifty-six years, eight months, and twenty-one days.[1] "

[1] Epitaph of Paula ; to Eustochium.

CHAPTER XXIV.

THE CONTROVERSY WITH AUGUSTINE.

A.D. 395-407.

ONE of the features of special interest in the life of Jerome is the way in which it makes us acquainted with nearly all the great Churchmen of his time. At the beginning of his career an accident only keeps Ambrose, the statesman bishop of Milan, off the scene at the Council of Rome, and Jerome seems never to have had any correspondence with him. Towards the close of his career he was prevented from entering into friendly relations with Chrysostom, the eloquent presbyter of Antioch, and bishop of Constantinople, by his sympathies with Paulinus of Antioch, and afterwards with Theodore of Alexandria and Epiphanius of Salamis, who were of the parties successively opposed to Chrysostom. But we find him in friendly relation with Basil of Cæsarea, Gregory Nazianzen, Theodore of Alexandria, and Augustine of Hippo. The relations between the two great fathers of the Latin Church are interesting, and characteristic enough to merit a little special attention.

Augustine was Jerome's junior in years, and still more his junior in the faith. Born at Tagaste, a city of Numidia, in the year 354 A.D., he had taught grammar and rhetoric in Carthage, then in Rome, and had afterwards accepted a professorship in those sciences in the public school of Milan. He had in youth adopted the tenets of the Manichæans, and had led an irregular life. He experienced the remarkable conversion which he relates in his "Confessions," and was baptized by Ambrose on the Easter Eve of 387. In the following year he returned to his native place, where he gave up his property to pious and charitable uses, and for nearly three years lived an ascetic and studious life. At the end of that time he was ordained a priest of the Church of Hippo, and four years afterwards Bishop of Hippo, where he exercised his episcopate for five-and-thirty years, the acknowledged leader of the African Church. He died 430 A.D. while Genseric and his Vandals were besieging his city.

The young bishop of Hippo and the aged recluse of the Cave of the Nativity had no personal acquaintance, but each was known to the other by reputation, and some formal letters, introducing travellers between the two countries, had passed between them. It was in the year 395 that a controversy arose between them which extended over the next twelve years.

We may briefly note the subject of the controversy, which is famous in the history of the Church, but we do not propose to trouble our readers with the argument. The subject was the dispute between St. Paul and St. Peter at Antioch, mentioned in the second chapter of Paul's Epistle to the Galatians, when St. Paul " withstood Peter to his face, because he was to be blamed " for yielding to the

Judaizing teachers who had come down from the Church of Jerusalem. Porphyry, the opponent of the faith in the middle of the third century, had taken advantage of this passage, to represent the Apostles as divided into opposite camps, and had represented St. Paul's conduct as "arrogant and impudent." The Eastern commentators maintained the theory that there was no real difference of opinion between the two Apostles, and that the scene between them had been arranged, in order in a striking manner to set at rest the dispute which was dividing the Antiochian Church.

Jerome, in his Commentary on the Epistle to the Galatians, written some years before, had adopted this explanation. His book fell into the hands of Augustine, to whom it seemed that this explanation of the scene at Antioch contradicted St. Paul, who plainly attributes vacillation to St. Peter, and represents his own rebuke as real; and moreover it attributed to the two Apostles a collusion which amounted to a "pious" fraud. The question seemed to Augustine of such importance that he addressed to Jerome a long letter in which he combated his views with all the power of his logical method, and with some sharpness of tone which might have been spared. The person to whom the letter was intrusted for conveyance to Jerome was prevented from making his projected journey to Bethlehem, and neglected either to forward it to its destination, or to return it to its writer. But in some way the letter got copied, and into circulation, as a work of Augustine's.

After some time Augustine finding that his letter

had not reached the hands of Jerome, wrote a second
letter on the same subject, still longer, more elaborate,
more incisive in its conclusions, and sharper in its
tone.   Unhappily, this letter met the same fate as
the first; it was not delivered by the messenger to
whom it was intrusted, but it got into circulation,
and only indirectly and after long delay came to the
knowledge of the person against whom it was
directed.

Some of Jerome's friends suggested that the rising
young theologian was seeking to increase his own
reputation by attacking that of the veteran scholar,
and was meanly keeping the attack from his knowledge that the silence of his antagonist might look
like an admission of his defeat.   Jerome was much
pained, and his friends at Bethlehem were very angry,
but he abstained from any communication with
Augustine on the subject.

Augustine, however, learnt from pilgrims passing
from Bethlehem to Hippo how matters stood, and
wrote to Jerome : " A rumour has reached me, which
I hesitate to believe, but why should I not mention
it to you ?   It has been told me that some of our
brothers, who are unknown to me, have given you to
understand that I have written a book against you,
and have sent it to Rome.   Believe me that it is
untrue, God is my witness that I have not done so.
If there is in any of my works anything which has
hurt you, tell me of it ; I shall receive your remarks
in a brotherly spirit, and shall find in them at the
same time the advantage of your corrections, and a
mark of your affection.   How happy I should be to

see you, to live near you, to assist at your conversations. But since God has deprived me of this favour, let me enjoy the only means which remains of uniting myself, in spite of distance, to you, and of living with you in Christ Jesus,—allow me to write to you, and do you answer me sometimes. Salute for me, my holy brother, Paulinian, and all the brothers, your companions, who boast of you, in the name of the Saviour. Remember me, my very dear lord, my most loved and honoured brother in Jesus Christ. May Christ fulfil all your desires, for which I earnestly pray."

This letter, conciliatory and affectionate in tone, was yet hardly satisfactory, since while denying that he had written a book against Jerome and sent it to Rome, it omitted all mention of the two letters which he had written against Jerome, and which had got into circulation in Rome and elsewhere. Jerome replied : " Most holy Lord and blessed Pope, a letter from your Blessedness reached me at the moment of the departure of our holy son, the sub-deacon Asterius, for the West. You affirm, in these lines which I read, that you have not sent a book written against me to Rome ; it is not a book which is in question, but a certain letter which is attributed to you, and of which our brother, Sysinnius, brought me a copy. You there exhort me to sing my palinode on the dispute of the Apostles, Peter and Paul, and to do like Stesichore, who changed his satire on Helen into panegyric, in order to recover his sight which he had lost through his misconduct. I sincerely admit that though I recognized in this writing your method of

argumentation and your style, I did not think I ought
rashly to accept its authenticity, and to reply to it, for
fear I might lay myself open to a charge of injustice
from your Blessedness, if I should attribute to you
what was not really yours.   To this reason for my
silence there is another, the long illness of the holy
and venerable Paula ; occupied entirely in solicitude
for her, I have almost forgotten your letter—or that
which has been circulated under your name.   Forgive
me for recalling to you the proverb, 'Music in
mourning is a tale out of season' (Ecclus. xxii. 6).   If
the writing is indeed yours, tell me so plainly, and
send me a copy of it, that we may discuss the Scriptures without bitterness, and learn either to correct
one another's errors, or to show one another that they
do not exist . . .   One thing remains for me to ask,
it is that you will love one who loves you, and that
you, a young man, will not provoke me, an old man,
to the battle-ground of the Scriptures.   We, too, have
had our day, we have held the lists with such force
as we had ; now that it is your turn to hold them,
and that you have obtained distinction, we claim
repose at your hands.   And that you may not be
alone when you invoke against me the fables of the
poets, recall to your mind Dares and Entellus.   Think
also of that proverb which says, 'When the ox is
weary, he puts down his feet more heavily.'   I dictate
these lines with grief.   Would to God that I might
have the happiness of embracing you, and that we
could converse together, in order that we might
understand one another, and teach one another
whatever we are ignorant of.

Q

" Remember me, holy and venerable Pope, and see
how I love you, I who, when provoked, have not been
willing to reply to you, and shrank from attributing
to you what I should have blamed in another."

Dares and Entellus are two athletes in the Æneid,
one young and confident, the other old, but full of
strength ; and the younger having provoked the elder
to the combat, got well beaten for his pains.

Augustine took great pains to soothe the suscep-
tibilities which he had provoked :—

"The letter which our holy son Asterius has brought
me from you," he says, " is harsh and affectionate at
the same time. In the most tender passages I see
tokens of displeasure, and I feel the point of a
reproach . . . But my very dear and well-beloved
brother, you would have feared to give me pain by
your reply, if my letter had not already given pain to
you, and you would not have sought to wound me if
you had not reason to think that I had first wounded
you. My only resource, under the circumstances, is
to acknowledge my fault, and to confess that the
letter which has offended you is really mine. Yes, I
have offended you, I conjure you by the mercy of
Jesus Christ not to render me evil for evil, by offending me in turn, but it would offend me if you did not
point out what you found reprehensible in my actions,
or in my words. You will not forget what the virtue
you profess, and the holy life you have embraced,
demand, viz., to condemn in me what your conscience
tells you is deserving of blame. Rebuke me then
with charity, if you think me blamable, or treat me
with the affection of a brother if I deserve your

affection.   In the first case I shall recognize in your
reprimands both my fault and your friendship.   Your
letters, a little too harsh, perhaps, but always salutary,
seem to me as redoubtable as the cestus of Entellus.
This aged athlete gave Dares terrible blows without
giving him health, he beat him without healing him.
As for me, if I receive your corrections with docility,
they will cure without hurting me.   I accept all your
comparisons, and since you wish it I see in you an
ox, yet an ox which labours with admirable success in
treading out the grain from the chaff on the thresh-
ing-floor of the Lord, and which, though ripe in years,
yet preserves all the vigour of youth ; behold me
stretched on the ground, tread me with all your
strength, I will bear with pleasure the weight which
your age gives you, provided the fault of which I am
guilty may be trodden out under your feet."

Jerome's rejoinder is a more full and elaborate
statement of his grievance.   "Most holy Lord and
well-beloved Pope, you have written me letters upon
letters to urge me to reply to a certain writing of
which the deacon Sysinnius brought me a copy without signature.   You affirm that you sent me this
writing, which indeed is addressed to me, first by our
brother Profuturus, and a second time by I know
not whom : and you add that Profuturus, being
elected bishop, and then dying suddenly, did not
come to Palestine ; while the other, whose name you
do not mention, changing his mind on the moment
of embarkation, remained on land out of fear of the
sea.   If that is so, I know not how to be sufficiently
astonished, how the letter in question should be in

everybody's hands at Rome and in Italy, so that the
deacon Sysinnius, my brother, found a copy five
years ago, not in your city, nor even in Africa, but in
an isle of the Adriatic.

" Friendship ought not to admit any suspicion, and
we ought to speak with a friend as with a second self.
I shall therefore tell you plainly that several of our
brothers, pure vessels of Christ, of whom there exists
a large number in Jerusalem and in the holy places,
suggested to me the idea that you have not acted in
all this matter with a sincere and upright spirit, but
that enamoured of praise, of applause, and of worldly
glory, you have sought the increase of your renown
in the diminishing of mine, acting in such a way that
many should suppose that you provoke and I shrink
back, that you write like a man of learning and I
hold my tongue like a fool, that at last I have found
some one who knows how to silence my loquacity.
I frankly avow to your Blessedness that this is the
reason which first of all hindered me from replying
to you ; next I hesitated to believe the letter yours,
thinking you incapable of attacking me, as the proverb, says ' With a sword smeared with honey' ; in
the third place, I feared that I might be accused of
arrogance towards a bishop if I should criticise my
critic a little sharply, especially when I meet in his
letter more than one passage which savours of
heresy. . . .

" You add, that if there is anything in your writings
which displeases me, and if I will correct it, you will receive my criticism in a brotherly spirit, and will see in
it a mark of my affection. Do you wish me to say what

I think without circumlocution ?   To propose such a
thing to me is to put scorn on an old man, it is to
force open the mouth of one who desires to hold his
tongue, it is to seek to make a vain parade of learning
at the cost of another.   Truly, if I undertook to
criticise you, the appearance it would have of un-
friendly envy of you, whose success ought to be so
dear to me, would suit ill with my age.   Meanwhile,
consider that the Gospel and the prophets are not
hidden from the criticism of perverse men, and do
not be astonished if one is able to find matter for
refutation in your books; above all, when you pretend
to explain the Scriptures, which are, as you know, so
full of difficulties.   Your works are scarce here.   I
have only been able to read of yours—and I hardly
know of any others—your Soliloquies and your Commentaries on the Psalms.   And if I chose to criticise
these latter, it would be easy for me to show that in
the explication or interpretation of texts, you are
not agreed, I do not say with me, who am nothing,
but with the doctors of the East, who are my masters.
Farewell, my very dear friend, my son in age, and my
father in dignity.   There is one thing more I wish to
ask ; it is this, when you are good enough to write to
me, take care that I am the first to receive your
letters !"

With this full expression of his grievances, and with
the good - humoured joke which concludes them,
Jerome seems to have dismissed all anger from his
mind, and then, in spite of all his disclaimers, he
plunges into the controversy to which Augustine had
invited him, and the two great theologians continued

it with an admirable display of their characteristic
turn of mind and literary style.

It must suffice here to say, that Jerome, having
begun with the foregone conclusion that the honour
of the Apostles is to be saved, shows great dialectical
skill in the establishment of his thesis. And that
Augustine, having begun with the conviction that
St. Paul's narrative must be taken quite literally, is
obliged to maintain the vacillation of Peter and the
"scandal" of Paul's open rebuke. The Eastern
Churches remained faithful to the traditional explanation which Jerome had championed. The
Western Church followed Augustine's view, and has
held ever since, that the Apostle, whose successor
claims a personal infallibility, first denied his Lord's
person and then his doctrine; exhibiting a grand
mixture of weakness and greatness, redeeming his
faults gloriously by his humility and his tears.

CHAPTER XXV.

THE FALL OF ROME,—FUGITIVES AT BETHLEHEM.

A.D. 406-418.

In the early part of this history we saw Rome at
the highest point of material splendour, wealth, and
luxury, and we were introduced to some of the
noblest families of its brilliant society; before the history closes we see it sacked by the barbarian hordes of
Alaric, its superb patriciate ruined, scattered, almost
annihilated; the history of ancient Rome concluded,
and that of Papal Rome begun.   The Northern
barbarians had long been pressing in threatening
hordes upon the frontiers.   Already, in 401, Alaric,
at the head of the Goths, had penetrated as far as
Venetia; in the following year he marched upon the
Imperial city, but was defeated by Stilicho at Pollentia,
and compelled to retreat.   In 406 Radagaisus
marched his mingled hordes across the defenceless
empire, till Florence, animated by Ambrose, arrested
the invaders before its walls, and Stilicho, cutting off
their supplies, and preventing their retreat, reduced
them to surrender.   In 408, 409, 410, Alaric again,
once, twice, and thrice threatened Rome.   The first
time he accepted a ransom, the second time the city
surrendered, and he placed a puppet emperor on the
throne, and marched to Ravenna to demand of
Honorius the confirmation of his title.   Being

refused, he retraced his steps to Rome, forced his way into the city, and the world heard, with horror and amazement, that the eternal city had been given up to sack by the barbarous Goths.

It was precisely to the class of nobles, to which the actors in our history chiefly belong, that the calamity was most fatal. Those palaces on the hills of Rome, where the aged Marcella gathered her assemblies of devotees, or where the heathen senator and Pontiff Albinus nursed his little grandchild; the palaces of Toxotius and Pammachius, and the rest in whose fate we have learned to take an interest; they were the special objects of the plunderer; that proud, refined, luxurious aristocracy were the greatest sufferers in the brutal horrors of a city delivered up to sack and pillage. How shall we tell the details of the horrors contained in the phrase "given up to sack and pillage"? The aged Marcella was put to the torture, scourged, trampled under foot, to make her reveal the hiding-place of the wealth which had long since been expended in building churches and hospitals, and feeding the poor; she died a few days afterwards. Pammachius died we know not how. Others disappeared, some under the charred ruins of their palaces, some under the Gothic swords, some under the hardships of their flight.

The inhabitants of the city and the provinces were everywhere hurrying from the ruins of the crumbling empire. They fled to the ports, and crowded every ship which sailed to Africa, to the East, to the islands, to any land which offered them a refuge. Many of the fugitives escaped from the barbarians only to

meet with treatment as barbarous from their countrymen.   The sailors robbed them on their voyage of
the valuables they had saved, and set them ashore
destitute ; the inhabitants of the countries where they
had been landed treated them as wreckers treat the
spoils of a shipwreck.   The provincial authorities
threw them into prison as vagabonds, in order to
extort a ransom.   Heraclianus, the count of Africa,
the friend of Augustine, is accused of having sold
noble maidens to a slave-dealer, who exposed them
for sale in the markets of Mesopotamia and Persia.
" No doubt," says Jerome, " everything which is born
is doomed to die, that which has matured must grow
old, there is no work of man but decay attacks it,
or age ends by destroying it.   But who would have
believed that Rome, raised by so many victories
above the universe, could one day crumble to pieces,
and be at once the mother and the tomb of her
people ?   That she who had reckoned the East, and
Egypt, and Africa among her slaves, should herself
become a slave in her turn ?   Who would have believed that obscure Bethlehem would see, begging at
its gates, nobles lately loaded with wealth ?   The
daughters of the queenly city now wander from shore
to shore, to Africa, to Egypt, to the East ; her ladies
have become servants ; the most illustrious personages ask bread at the gate of Bethlehem, and
when we cannot give it to them all, we give them, at
least, our tears.   In vain I try to snatch myself from
the sight of such sufferings by resuming my unfinished work, I am incapable of study.   I feel that
this is the time for translating the precepts of Scrip-

ture not into words but into deeds, and not for saying holy things but doing them."[1] The communities of Bethlehem did what they could in the midst of this misery. Eustochium received as many women as she could into her three monasteries, Jerome received the men, the guest-house relieved others.

Among these fugitives were two who caused a terrible grief and scandal among the religious of Bethlehem. It is right to record it, in order not to conceal the fact that these early religious houses did not escape the dangers to which such communities are liable, but we need not dwell upon the story. A young deacon, Sabinianus, presented himself at Bethlehem; he had an elegant appearance, pleasing manners, a fine voice, and good recommendations;

---

[1] Ezech. iii. Prefat. Jerome's letters afford several individual examples of the sufferings of the people from the Barbarians. To Julianus, a noble and rich Spaniard, who had lost by sudden death two young daughters and his wife :—"They tell me also that this misfortune has been followed by the loss of your goods; that, in the pillage of the province by the Barbarians, your fields have been ravaged, your flocks carried off, your slaves killed or taken." To Rusticus, a Gaul :—He and his wife had been "obliged to separate, in order to escape the fury of the Barbarians and the danger of falling into slavery." She had sought refuge in the Holy Land, and devoted herself to a religious life. He had promised to follow her. Jerome writes, at her request, to remind him of his promise and urge him to fulfil it : "But if the ruins of your house still detain you, if you wish to witness the death of your friends and fellow-citizens, if you wish to see the ruin and desolation of cities and villages, at least take penitence as a plank to cling to amidst the shipwreck of your province, and to arm you against the cruelty of the Barbarians and the miseries of captivity."

Jerome received him, and attached him as a Reader to the staff of the Church of the Nativity. It was afterwards found out that the young Roman had had an intrigue at Rome with the wife of one of the Gallic chiefs, that they were surprised by the husband, the wife was slain, the lover escaped, fled to Syria, received the diaconate, and finally presented himself at Bethlehem. This man had gained the affections of one of the nuns of Eustochium, and had made preparations for her escape from the window of the convent, for their flight to the coast, and for their passage across the sea. The intrigue was, however, discovered. The nun was secured in her cell; Sabinianus professed penitence, and sought Jerome's forgiveness, but took an early opportunity to make his escape ; and then revenged himself by assailing Jerome with insults and spreading calumnies about the monasteries of Bethlehem. A letter of Jerome addressed to this man is the authority for the story. It is a letter, by the way, very different in tone from what we should have expected from Jerome. Instead of scourging the man with bitter invectives, he calmly reasons with him, and tries to bring him to a sense of sin and to repentance.

Another of the fugitives brought with him the seeds of a new heresy, which gradually spread into all branches of the Church. This was the heresiarch Pelagius, a native of Wales, his name being, according to a British tradition, Morgan, of which Pelagius is the Greek equivalent. He was a man of great learning and eloquence, and if we accept the calm opinion of Augustine in preference to the prejudiced vituperation of Jerome, a man of high character for piety and virtue. He had conceived some novel opinions, the chief of which were on the nature of man's free will and God's grace, and the relations between them. He held that men did not inherit Adam's fallen nature, but that in which he was created ; and, consequently, that God's preventing grace was not necessary—though His providential assistance was—to enable men to live a holy life.

Pelagius had appeared in Rome about the year 405, and had obtained considerable reputation among that society of noble Christians of which we have already heard so much. Among his disciples was Celestius, a skilful advocate, who carried Pelagius's doctrines to greater lengths than his master.

The political troubles of Rome drove both master and disciple to seek refuge in Africa. Pelagius did not remain there long, but went on to Palestine ; Celestius remained in Africa, and was brought before a synod at Carthage, which condemned and excommunicated him. The attention of Jerome was attracted to the controversy, and he wrote a treatise, in the form of a letter to Ctesiphon, against the new doctrines, without however mentioning the name of Pelagius.

When Pelagius himself appeared at Jerusalem in 415, he was well received by the bishop John, and his teaching was received by the clergy of that Church. The disputations of the Eastern Church had all turned upon the nature of God and the relations of the Divine and human natures in Christ ; and the field of discussion presented, in human nature and the relations of its native powers to the influences of the Holy Spirit, was at once novel and foreign to the genius of the Eastern Church. It was to the West that this new controversy belonged, as the earlier disputes had belonged to the East.

The Western opponents of Pelagianism had followed Pelagius to Jerusalem, and carried on a resolute opposition to his doctrines. Jerome's Latin mind and Western connections led him to entertain a deep interest in the question, and to take his part with the opposition to Pelagius. A Synod of the Church of Jerusalem was held on the subject under the presidency of Bishop John, and Pelagius made some general and ambiguous statements which satisfied the assembly of his orthodoxy. His opponents, however, procured the examination of the question before the higher tribunal of a Council of the Bishops of Palestine under the Metropolitan of Cæsarea, and again the explanations of Pelagius were received as satisfactory. This was a great triumph to Pelagius and his friends. The affair had excited much popular interest; party feeling ran high, and the Anti-Pelagians were insulted when they appeared in the streets. Jerome, and the monasteries of Bethlehem, which still resolutely maintained their attitude of antagonism, became a mark for the popular indignation. One night a mob of partizans went down from Jerusalem and made an attack upon the convents of Bethlehem. One party attacked the monastery of men, where the monks defended themselves successfully. Another party attacked the monasteries of women, forced the doors, and set fire to the buildings.

The majority of the nuns, escorted by the servants of the monastery, fled, and sought by a circuit to gain the protection of the tower which had been erected at one end of the pile of buildings to serve as a citadel in case of attack from the wild tribes of Arabs. Jerome and his monks made a sally, and covered the retreat of the women ; the inhabitants of the village, roused by the tumult, also came to the rescue of the religious ; and the assailants were finally driven off, but not before there had been much bloodshed on both sides, nor before the women's monasteries had been plundered and partially burnt.

The shock of this wild night probably hastened the end of Eustochium, whose health had long been declining. We have no account from Jerome of her last moments, such as that which he gave of her mother's. All we know is that she passed away as into a gentle sleep, on the 28th of September, 418, sixteen years after the death of her mother, and was buried near her in the rocky crypt beneath the Church of the Nativity. The younger Paula, the daughter of Toxotius, assumed the direction of the monasteries.

CHAPTER XXVI.

THE DEATH OF JEROME.

A.D. 418–420.

OUR history concludes, like some great tragedy, with the deaths, not only of the hero, but of all the principal persons in whom we have taken an interest.

Jerome survived most of his friends. He had laid the funeral wreath of an elogium successively on the tombs of Damasus, Blesilla, Albina, Asella, Nepotian, Heliodorus, Lucinus, Fabiola, Paula, Pammachius, Marcella, Eustochium. He had survived foes as well as friends. Rufinus, driven out of his retreat at Aquileia by the invasion of the Goths, took refuge in Sicily, and died there in 410 A.D. We grieve to have to record the bitter words in which Jerome exulted over his former adversary :—" The scorpion is buried under the soil of Sicily with Enceladus and Porphyrion; the many-headed hydra has ceased to hiss against us."

John of Jerusalem died about A.D. 416.

Thus, in the midst, as it were, of the ruins of the Empire, and the graves of friends and foes, the old man lingered for two years in sickness and sorrow. The full stream of his literary productiveness ceased to flow, the torrent of his invective was dried up. By the help of a cord fixed to the ceiling of his cell he used to raise himself on his couch while he recited his Hours; his sight, we know, had long been defective; his voice faded to a whisper; his body became so

thin as to seem almost transparent. The younger
Paula, the child of Toxotius and grandchild of
Paula, the child dedicated before her birth to the life
of a Church-virgin, whom Jerome had trained and
educated with paternal solicitude, now soothed his
last days with filial care.

One of the many legends which gathered in after
years about his name relates that Augustine admini-
stered the last sacrament to him. One of the great
paintings of the world—the Last Sacrament of Jerome
by Domenichino—gives us a striking representation
of the legend, which we gladly accept as the last scene
in the history of the first great father of the Western
Church.

He died on the 30th of September, in the year
420 A.D., at about the age of seventy-four, having lived
the last thirty-four years of his life in his monastery at
Bethlehem.

The visitor to Bethlehem descends from the choir
into the crypt beneath, to worship at the Cave of the
Nativity. A passage cut through the rock leads him
thence through various rock chambers to the cell which
Jerome called his Paradise, the scene of thirty years
of literary labours, where aged Paula and youthful
Eustochium read and discussed the holy Scriptures
with him, where the scribes waited, with uplifted eye
and pen, for the copious flow of his words, where the
Biblia Vulgata was written. In an adjoining cell are
two sepulchres, one is that of Jerome, the other that
of Paula and Eustochium.

RICHARD CLAY & SONS, LIMITED, LONDON & BUNGAY.

PUBLICATIONS

OF THE

Society for Promoting Christian Knowledge.

THE

FATHERS FOR ENGLISH READERS.

A Series of Monographs on the Chief Fathers of the Church.

Fcap. 8vo., cloth boards, 2s. each.

BONIFACE.
By the Rev. I. GREGORY SMITH, M.A. (1s. 6d.).

LEO THE GREAT.
By the Rev. CANON GORE, M.A.

GREGORY THE GREAT.
By the Rev. J. BARMBY, B.D.

SAINT AMBROSE: his Life, Times, and Teaching.
By the Ven. ARCHDEACON THORNTON, D.D.

SAINT ATHANASIUS: his Life and Times.
By the Rev. R. WHELER BUSH (2s. 6d.).

SAINT AUGUSTINE.
By the Rev. E. L. CUTTS, D.D.

SAINT BASIL THE GREAT.
By the Rev. RICHARD T. SMITH, B.D.

SAINT BERNARD: Abbot of Clairvaux, A.D. 1091—1153.
By the Rev. S. J. EALES, M.A., D.C.L. (2s. 6d.).

SAINT HILARY OF POITIERS, AND SAINT MARTIN OF TOURS.
By the Rev. J. GIBSON CAZENOVE, D.D.

SAINT JEROME.
By the Rev. EDWARD L. CUTTS, D.D.

SAINT JOHN OF DAMASCUS.
By the Rev. J. H. LUPTON, M.A.

SAINT PATRICK: his Life and Teaching.
By the Rev. E. J. NEWELL, M.A. (2s. 6d.).

SYNESIUS OF CYRENE, Philosopher and Bishop.
By ALICE GARDNER.

THE APOSTOLIC FATHERS.
By the Rev. CANON SCOTT-HOLLAND.

THE DEFENDERS OF THE FAITH; or, The Christian Apologists of the Second and Third Centuries.
By the Rev. F. WATSON, D.D.

THE VENERABLE BEDE.
By the Right Rev. G. F. BROWNE, D.D.

Non-Christian Religious Systems.

Fcap. 8vo., cloth boards, 2s. 6d. each.

Buddhism: Being a Sketch of the Life and Teachings of Gautama, the Buddha.
By T. W. RHYS DAVIDS, M.A., Ph.D. With Map.

Buddhism in China.
By the late Rev. S. BEAL. With Map.

Christianity and Buddhism: a Comparison and a Contrast.
By the Rev. T. STERLING BERRY, D.D.

Confucianism and Taouism.
By Professor DOUGLAS, of the British Museum. With Map.

Hinduism.
By Sir M. MONIER WILLIAMS, M.A., D.C.L. With Map.

Islam and its Founder.
By J. W. H. STOBART. With Map.

Islam as a Missionary Religion.
By CHARLES R. HAINES (2s.).

The Coran: Its Composition and Teaching, and the Testimony it bears to the Holy Scriptures.
By Sir WILLIAM MUIR, K.C.S.I., LL.D., D.C.L., Ph.D.

The Religion of the Crescent, or Islam; its Strength, its Weakness, its Origin, its Influence.
By the Rev. W. St. CLAIR-TISDALL, M.A. (4s.)

The Heathen World and St. Paul.

Fcap. 8vo., cloth boards, 2s. each.

St. Paul in Greece.
By the Rev. G. S. DAVIES. With Map.

St. Paul in Damascus and Arabia.
By the Rev. G. RAWLINSON, M.A. With Map.

St. Paul at Rome.
By the late Very Rev. C. MERIVALE, D.D., D.C.L. With Map.

St. Paul in Asia Minor and at the Syrian Antioch.
By the late Rev. E. H. PLUMPTRE, D.D. With Map.

The Home Library.

A Series of Books illustrative of Church History, &c., specially, but not exclusively, adapted for Sunday reading.

Crown 8vo., cloth boards, 3s. 6d. each.

Black and White. Mission Stories.
By the late H. A. FORDE.

Charlemagne.
By the Rev. E. L. CUTTS, D.D. With Map.

Constantine the Great: The Union of Church and State.
By the Rev. EDWARD L. CUTTS, D.D.

John Hus. The Commencement of Resistance to Papal Authority on the part of the Inferior Clergy.
By the Rev. A. H. WRATISLAW.

Judæa and her Rulers, from Nebuchadnezzar to Vespasian.
By M. BRAMSTON. With Map.

Mazarin.
By the late GUSTAVE MASSON.

Military Religious Orders of the Middle Ages: the Hospitallers, the Templars, the Teutonic Knights, and others.
By the Rev. F. C. WOODHOUSE.

Mitslav; or, the Conversion of Pomerania.
By the late Right Rev. R. MILMAN, D.D.

Narcissus: A Tale of Early Christian Times.
By the Right Rev. W. BOYD CARPENTER.

Richelieu.
By the late GUSTAVE MASSON.

Sketches of the Women of Christendom.
By the late MRS. RUNDLE CHARLES.

The Churchman's Life of Wesley.
By R. DENNY URLIN Esq

THE HOME LIBRARY (*Continued*).

The Church in Roman Gaul.
By the Rev. R. T. SMITH. With Map.

The House of God the Home of Man.
By the Rev. Canon JELF.

The Inner Life, as Revealed in the Correspondence of Celebrated Christians.
Edited by the late Rev. T. ERSKINE.

The Life of the Soul in the World: Its Nature, Needs, Dangers, Sorrows, Aids, and Joys.
By the Rev. F. C. WOODHOUSE.

The North African Church.
By the late Rev. J. LLOYD. With Map.

Thoughts and Characters: being Selections from the Writings of the late MRS. RUNDLE CHARLES.

Conversion of the West.

A Series of Volumes showing how the Conversion of the Chief Races of the West was brought about, and their condition before this occurred.

Fcap. 8vo., cloth boards, 2s. each.

The Celts.
By the Rev. G. F. MACLEAR, D.D. With Two Maps.

The English.
By the above Author. With Two Maps.

The Northmen.
By the above Author. With Map.

The Slavs.
By the above Author. With Map.

The Continental Teutons.
By the late Very Rev. Dean MERIVALE. With Map.

Devotional Books.

Cheerful Christianity. Having to do with the Lesser Beauties and Blemishes of the Christian Life. By L. B. WALFORD. Printed in red and black. Post 8vo., cloth boards, 1s. 6d.

[For devotional reading, &c.]

The Gospel of Suffering. By Mrs. COLIN G. CAMPBELL, Author of "Bible Thoughts for Daily Life." Post 8vo., cloth boards, 1s.

[Shows the significance of our Lord's teaching as to sorrow. For general use.]

Our Own Book. Very plain reading for people in humble life By the Rev. F. BOURDILLON, M.A. Post 8vo., cloth boards, 1s.

[A devotional work, in large type. For the poor.]

Plain Words for Christ. By the late Rev. R. G. DUTTON. Being a series of Readings for Working Men. Post 8vo., 1s.

[These readings have to do with very important subjects, which are dealt with in a simple and striking manner.]

Spiritual Counsels; or, Helps and Hindrances to Holy Living. By the late Rev. R. G. DUTTON, M.A. Post 8vo., cloth boards, 1s.

[Addresses to young men on points of spiritual interest.]

Thoughts for Men and Women. The Lord's Prayer. By EMILY C. ORR. Post 8vo., 1s.

[Simple and suggestive thoughts on the Lord's Prayer.]

Thoughts for Working Days. Original and selected. By EMILY C. ORR. Post 8vo., 1s.

[A series of daily readings for a month, in which the path of duty is marked out by selections from the writings of celebrated men.]

The Message of Peace, and other Christmas Sermons. By the late R. W. CHURCH, Dean of St. Pauls. Crown 8vo., on "hand-made" paper, top edge gilt, buckram boards, 2s. 6d.

[Eight striking Sermons on the Nativity. Full of deep and suggestive thought.]

The True Vine. By the late MRS. RUNDLE CHARLES. With border-lines in red. Post 8vo., cloth boards, 1s. 6d.

[Thoughts on the Parable of the True Vine. For devotional use.]

Miscellaneous Publications.

Bible Places; or, the Topography of the Holy Land: a Succinct Account of all the Places, Rivers, and Mountains of the Land of Israel mentioned in the Bible, so far as they have been identified. Together with their Modern Names and Historical References. By the Rev. Canon TRISTRAM. New Edition brought up to date. Crown 8vo. With Map and numerous Woodcuts. Cloth boards, 5s.

China. By Professor R. K. DOUGLAS, of the British Museum. With Map, and eight full-page Illustrations, and several Vignettes. Post 8vo., cloth boards, 5s.

Christians under the Crescent in Asia. By the Rev. E. L. CUTTS, D.D., Author of "Turning Points of Church History," &c. With numerous Illustrations. Post 8vo., cloth boards, 5s.

Higher Criticism (The) and the Verdict of the Monuments. By the Rev. A. H. SAYCE, Professor of Assyriology, Oxford. Demy 8vo., buckram, bevelled boards, 7s. 6d.

History of Early Christian Art. By the Rev. E. L. CUTTS, D.D. Illustrated. Demy 8vo., cloth boards, 6s.

Illustrated Notes on English Church History. Vol. I. From the earliest Times to the Reformation. Vol. II Reformation and Modern Work. By the Rev. C. A. LANE. With numerous Illustrations. Crown 8vo., cloth boards, each, 1s.

Israel, The Land of. A Journal of Travels in Palestine, undertaken with Special Reference to its Physical Character. Fourth Edition, revised. By the Rev. Canon TRISTRAM. With numerous Illustrations. Cloth boards, 10s. 6d.

Jewish Nation, A History of the. From the Earliest Times to the Present Day. By the late E. H. PALMER. Crown 8vo. With Map and numerous Illustrations. Cloth boards, 4s.

Lesser Lights; or, Some of the Minor Characters of Scripture traced with a View to Instruction and Example in Daily Life. By the Rev. F. BOURDILLON, M.A. First and Second Series. Post 8vo., cloth boards, each, 2s. 6d.; Third Series, 2s.

Natural History of the Bible, The : being a Review of the Physical Geography, Geology, and Meteorology of the Holy Land, with a description of every Animal and Plant mentioned in Holy Scripture. By the Rev. Canon TRISTRAM. Crown 8vo. With numerous Illustrations. Cloth boards, 5s.

Official Year Book of the Church of England. Demy 8vo., paper boards, 3s. ; limp cloth, 4s.

Patriarchal Palestine. By the Rev. A. H. SAYCE, Professor of Assyriology, Oxford. Crown 8vo., with Map, buckram boards, 4s.

Pictorial Architecture of France. By the Rev. H. H. BISHOP, M.A. With numerous Illustrations. Royal 4to., cloth boards, 7s. 6d.

Pictorial Architecture of the British Isles. By the Rev. H. H. BISHOP. With about 150 Illustrations. Royal 4to., cloth boards, 4s.

Pictorial Architecture of Greece and Italy. By the Rev. H. H. BISHOP. With numerous Illustrations. Royal 4to., cloth boards, 5s.

Pictorial Geography of the British Isles. By MARY E. PALGRAVE. With numerous Illustrations. Royal 4to., cloth boards, 5s.

Russia, Past and Present. Adapted from the German of Lankenau and Oelnitz. By Mrs. CHESTER. With Map and three full-page Woodcuts and Vignettes. Post 8vo., cloth boards, 5s.

Scripture Manners and Customs : being an Account of the Domestic Habits, Arts, &c., of Eastern Nations mentioned in Holy Scripture. Twentieth Edition. Crown 8vo. With numerous Woodcuts. Cloth boards, 4s.

Sinai and Jerusalem ; or, Scenes from Bible Lands, consisting of Coloured Photographic Views of Places mentioned in the Bible, including a Panoramic View of Jerusalem. With Descriptive Letterpress by the Rev. F. W. Holland, M.A. 4to., cloth, bevelled boards, gilt edges, 6s.

Some Notable Archbishops of Canterbury. By the Rev. MONTAGUE FOWLER, M.A. Crown 8vo., cloth boards, 3s.

Turning Points of English Church History. By the Rev. EDWARD L. CUTTS, D.D. Crown 8vo., cloth boards, 3s. 6d.

Turning Points of General Church History. By the Rev. E. L. CUTTS, D.D. Crown 8vo., cloth boards, 4s.

Verses. By the late CHRISTINA G. ROSSETTI. Small post 8vo. Printed in red and black. Cloth boards, 3s. 6d.

ANCIENT HISTORY FROM THE MONUMENTS.

[*This series of books is chiefly intended to illustrate the Sacred Scriptures by the results of recent Monumental researches in the East.*]

Fcap. 8vo., cloth boards, price 2s. each.

ASSYRIA, FROM THE EARLIEST TIMES TO THE FALL OF NINEVEH.

By the late GEORGE SMITH, of the Department of Oriental Antiquities, British Museum.

BABYLONIA, THE HISTORY OF.

By the late GEORGE SMITH. Edited and brought up to date by the Rev. Professor SAYCE.

PERSIA, FROM THE EARLIEST PERIOD TO THE ARAB CONQUEST.

By the late W. S. W. VAUX, M.A., F.R.S. A New and Revised Edition, by the Rev. Professor A. H. SAYCE.

SINAI, FROM THE FOURTH EGYPTIAN DYNASTY TO THE PRESENT DAY.

By the late H. SPENCER PALMER. A New Edition, revised throughout by the Rev. Professor SAYCE.

LONDON : NORTHUMBERLAND AVENUE, W.C.

43, QUEEN VICTORIA STREET, E.C.